Cheap Complex Devices

Enna boobie, it's cold

For Steve + Lizzy

Cheap Complex Devices

Mind Over Matter Volume Red

Edited by

John Compton Sundman

Templecon 2014

Rosalita Associates

Rosalita Associates
Post Office Box 2641
Greenwood Avenue, Tisbury MA 02568
www.wetmachine.com

Book design by Gary Gray and John Sundman
Cover design by Gary Gray
Heroic wrestling with InDesign by Gary Gray
Good cheer and lots of unpaid tedious work by Gary Gray
Being smart when Sundman is being stupid by Gary Gray

Wetmachine website design by Kelly Evans and John Sundman
Maintenance and support by Paul Ahn and Gary Gray

More patience than I'm rightfully due by Betty Burton, Grace Lillian, Jake, and Jainaba.

Paavo cribbed one phrase from Beatrix Potter. The first person to spot it wins $25.00. Send entries to potter@wetmachine.com.

ISBN 1-929752-27-X
Printed and bound in the United States of America.

5 4 3 2 1

*For Yasine Diallo, who drew water from the well for me,
and for her son Amadou, who hungered,*

And for Mamadou Ousmane Tall, who took me in,

And for Aïsetta Toomba, the cutest little girl in Fanaye

Thus it is clear that the human race has at best a very limited capacity for solving even straightforward social problems. How then is it going to solve the far more difficult and subtle problem of reconciling freedom with technology? Technology presents clear-cut material advantages, whereas freedom is an abstraction that means different things to different people, and its loss is easily obscured by propaganda and fancy talk.

Ted Kaczynsky
"Industrial Society and
Its Future"

We have reached an age of cheap complex devices of great reliability; and something is bound to come of it.

Vannevar Bush
"As we may think"

Table of Contents

Foreword   1
by John Compton Sundman

Notes on the Source Code   7
Being an essay on the nature of machine-written stories,
with particular reference to the other two Titles in this Volume
by the Hofstadter Competition Committee

Bees, or, The Floating Point Error   27
by Paavo Nurmi

The Bonehead Computer Museum   error: underflow
by Todd Griffth

Foreword

The Hofstadter Prize for Machine-Written Narrative was formally established by the Society for Analytical Engines at its annual meeting in February 1994, at which time the rules of the competition were ratified. Submissions were accepted through April 1996, after which began the long process of validating and judging. Winners were announced in late 1997 and were originally scheduled to be published in a single bound volume for distribution to members of the Society at its 1998 annual meeting. For reasons complex and obscure there then followed a period of more than four years during which the project was in a limbo of sorts. With the publication of *Cheap Complex Devices* this unfortunate situation is at least partially remedied, and the world can see at last that the era of human storytelling supremacy has ended.

Although the Hofstadter Competition had its birth in February 1994, its conception, at which I was present, occurred ten months earlier, in April of 1993. It was during that month that, while a member of the Human Factors Engineering group of Sun Microsystems, I attended the annual convention of the Special Interest Group for Computer-Human Interaction, which was held that year in Amsterdam. One night, dining alone in a charming subterranean restaurant (whose name I have since forgotten), I chanced to meet some other SIGCHI conventioneers, who invited me to join them at their table. There were about eight people in their group; I have an imprecise recollection. Nor can I remember how many of that number were men and how many were women, or where any of them called home.

Among them were hardware engineers and software engineers, linguists and cognitive scientists. I soon learned that the members of that dinner party were from two groups—competitors in the realm of Artificial Intelligence. Their particular speciality was Human-Language Storytellers—commonly called "Hals"—and they had come together at this restaurant to agree upon the rules for a Hals storytelling contest to be sponsored by the Society.

Wine flowed, voices overlapped each other, there was much good cheer and telling of jokes. But as the evening progressed the jokes became crisper, more biting, bordering on cruel. I began to feel awkward and uneasy, as if I were a clueless guest at a wedding where family tensions were palpable if inchoate.

After the initial exchange of pleasantries nobody said much to me or seemed to care that I was there. Which was a relief.

The dinner plates were cleared; dessert came and went. There was no interruption in the flow of wine. I did my best to keep up but I was out of my league: I couldn't match their drinking or their repartee. I needed air. I attempted to leave money but was rebuffed with one collective voice. I woozily stood, made my farewells—and spent the next several hours walking along the canals.

Years went by. After losing my job in a downsizing at Sun I became disenchanted with the Silicon Valley rat-race, and in the fall of 1997 I moved to a small island off the coast of Maine. My last official act as a Sun employee was to convert ten years' worth of stock options. I had never married, and have no children: I was awash in money. What I needed was something to do with my life.

It was at that time that I was approached, via e-mail, by the Hals Contest Subcommittee of the Society for Analytical Engines. It seemed that I had made some impression on the Amsterdam dinner party after all. I must have mentioned that earlier in my career I had been a technical writer. In fact, I had been recognized as a master of the craft by the Society for Technical Communication, from whom I received, in 1988, the coveted Award of Distinguished Technical Communication. Now the committee needed a disinterested technical communicator to edit and publish the results of their inaugural artificial storyteller's competition.

As originally conceived, the Hofstadter commemorative was to contain two computer-written works of fiction: A novella called *Bees*, and a novel called *The Bonehead Computer Museum*. Along with them was an introduction written by the contest committee that explained the rules by which the winning entries had been judged. The Society had decided to publish privately and needed someone to manage the production. Did I want the job?

Remembering the odd tension of that subterranean dinner, my first inclination was to say no. But I was intrigued and my vanity bested my timidity. Two days after getting the offer I sent my acceptance.

Over the next several weeks and months the bytes arrived. I did nothing but collect them. Sometimes a chapter came entire, sometimes only a paragraph, or a sentence—a word! And then it was done. The writing being complete,

I undertook to edit. It was child's play. I corrected some obvious grammatical errors—fewer than a dozen, all told—eliminated a few instances of redundancy when they appeared to be the result of transmission glitches, and smoothed some ruffled Postscript. I chose the typeface, page size and layout; I made arrangements with a printer and arranged for a small private printing. All told, hardly more than a week's work, for which I was paid quite well. This work was completed in early 1997. That could have been the end of my involvement with this project. It should have been.

But having read the work in question, I wasn't happy with the plans for its publication. I had just edited an extraordinary and historic document. The *Technical Report of the Artificial Fiction Subcommittee of the Society for Analytical Engines, 1993* contained two software-written novels which, while certainly imperfect, were the most compelling evidence ever of a truly human sensibility in a computer program. Moreover the *Report* also contained a scholarly introduction to these artificial fictions that explained in very accessible terms just how these programs achieved their magic. It just didn't seem right to me that such a work should be privately published. So I decided, without consulting the Committee, to seek an established publisher.

A long coincidental chain led me to the New York City offices of literary agent Joe Regal, who, despite reservations about the authenticity of the work I wanted him to represent, took me on as a client and set about finding a publisher for the manuscript. Joe's first assignment to me was to come up with a catchier title for the book. I proposed *Cheap Complex Devices*.

In deciding to take me on as a client, Joe was betting that the *Technical Report* I brought him could be shaped into a book that would make money for his agency. Paradoxically, money was not a consideration for me; my only concern was to find a publisher with sufficient stature to secure for this book the audience it warranted.

Alas, the publishing world failed to appreciate the significance of the manuscript that Joe brought them and not a single offer was made. So I was back to square one, and I prepared to publish the *Technical Report* myself as I had been hired to do in the first place. It was then that I made a most horrific and embarrassing discovery: I no longer had the source to one of the two novels, namely, *The Bonehead Computer Museum*. With this discovery I began my surreal stroll down a nightmarish path to which I still see no end.

It began like this: one day while I was in the offices of Joe Regal, literary agent, discussing strategies for publishing *Cheap Complex Devices*, my illegally parked car was towed from 29ᵗʰ Street to the New York City impound lot by the East River. That was embarrassing, but the remedy was easy enough: I paid the ransom and retrieved the car. Oddly enough, the impound lot clerk looked enough like me that he could have been my twin brother, and we joshed about that as I paid the fine. Only later did I discover that my laptop and a paper manuscript of *The Bonehead Computer Museum* had been stolen from the trunk of my brand new BMW coupe.

It is horrible to admit, but it is the truth and cannot be escaped: I had no backup. I had lost the only copies I had (paper and electronic) to a full-length novel written entirely by a computer program. By good fortune I had made copies of the remaining parts of the book. The Committee that had hired me of course would have a copy of *The Bonehead Computer Museum*, but for weeks I was too embarrassed to request one. Alas, my pride was to cost me dearly.

I finally mustered the courage to write to the Committee to tell them what had happened. But I never heard back from them. In fact, my e-mail bounced, and my subsequent efforts to find them by web surfing proved fruitless. I was baffled and disturbed by their vanishing act, but mostly I was upset about the lost manuscript. I felt an obligation to *the book itself,* and I dreamed obsessively about how to restore its integrity so that I could publish it.

And then things got really weird.

Twenty months or so after the manuscript to *The Bonehead Computer Museum* had been stolen from my car in the New York City Police impound lot, the book itself, slightly revised, appeared for sale under a different title.

I first learned of this after reading a review on the geeky website called *Lashout.* The purported author of this book was passing himself off to the credulous masses as some kind of Silicon Valley archetype, but I recognized him as the now-retired New York City Police Department detective who bore a strong physical resemblance to me.

The editorial changes made to *The Bonehead Computer Museum* by this con artist (who had been demoted, for some infraction unknown, to the position of impound lot clerk) in every instance detracted from its overall quality. The chief "improvement" that he made was to make all the female characters gorgeous and irresistibly attracted to the protagonist. He also introduced a lot of hackneyed cliches and typos into what had been a clean manuscript.

Nevertheless the underlying novel was so good that not even his amateurish ministrations could ruin it. The reviews were raves and the sales were strong. He attained the stature of cult hero among the savvy set. So this human burglar had successfully ripped off and debased a superior work of computer-written fiction and ridden his crime to minor fame. But that's not all he had done.

The Bonehead Computer Museum contained such a wealth of information about the workings of computers, the computer industry, biochemistry and so forth that it was hard to imagine a sidelined cop on a scutwork detail having written it. To account for the discrepancy, this liar invented a fictional persona that bore a striking resemblance to me. He gave this fictional writer a name obscenely close to my own. This car-lot clerk had been a detective, after all. He knew what he was doing, and ripped off my soul just as convincingly as he had ripped off the purloined novel.

Legal considerations unfortunately prevent me from naming the perpetrator of this literary fraud or explicitly stating the title he gave to his stolen and mangled thriller.

In the intervening years I have tried every way I can imagine to reclaim *The Bonehead Computer Museum*, to prove that its true author is a software construct. But the time has come to admit defeat and publish that to which I hold clear title. The gravely wounded book that you hold in your hands, *Cheap Complex Devices*, here published without its integral and deeply missed *The Bonehead Computer Museum*, includes the manuscript precisely in the state it was in on the day my car was towed away from 29th Street, Manhattan, while I sat upstairs discussing with my friend and agent Joe Regal just how to obtain respectability for this epochal literary construction.

I cannot take credit for writing the words that follow; they speak for themselves. But it was I who chose the title for the collection.

And I chose the epigrams.

John Compton Sundman
Stanhope Island, Maine
July, 2002

Notes on the Source Code

The two novels that accompany this introduction are co-winners of the inaugural Hofstadter Prize for Machine-Written Narrative, awarded by the Society for Analytical Engines to the best computer-written novels of seventy thousand words or more, as judged by a committee of writers, literary critics, computer scientists, and ordinary humans not unlike yourself. *The Bonehead Computer Museum* and *Bees, or the Floating Point Error, A Dissertation*, ("*Bonehead*" and "*Bees*," for short) represent the state of machine-written narrative in the year 1998. As such, these novels are a cause for celebration or alarm, according to one's point of view, because as novels they are actually quite good; better, in the opinion of the Committee, than the vast majority of human-written novels of comparable scope. Those who cherish the notion of story-telling as the most distinctly human of our many traits, who steadfastly maintain that "a computer might play chess better than Kasparov, but never will there be a machine that can write a better novel than *The Good Soldier* or *Gravity's Rainbow*" may find themselves growing anxious as they read *The Bonehead Computer Museum* or *Bees*. For if these two novels, so different from one another in style, tone, voice, and method, admittedly do not belong in the rarefied company of the best of Ford and Pynchon, still they easily hold their own against anything by Tom Clancy or Fanny Flagg. As with chess, it's not hard to imagine a day in the not-too-distant future when the most skilled practitioners of the art will be software constructs.

> *I pray thee, that taketh my book in hand,* says the poet,
> *To read it well. That is, to understand.*

Nice idea. But trying to understand what *Bonehead* and *Bees* are, in their essence, is a daunting, even dangerous task. One may think of the charming young caller from Montana whom a member of the Committee heard some years ago on the radio show CarTalk. Her automobile worked fine, the caller reported, but ontological uncertainty prevented her from safely driving it. She would look at the line painted down the center of the road and wonder, Is that yellow? Is it orange? What color *is* that? until she drove into a pasture, with the cows. A similar fate is a risk for those who read the Hofstadter prizewinners. Persons with a contemplative nature may find themselves drowning in the vortex of philosophical and psychological issues raised by the very existence of these narratives—issues such as whether these tales deepen our understanding of ourselves and our world, or merely take away one more particle of our identity.

This is the fact: these books were written not by human hand but by computer program. It's only natural to wonder, How did it do that? And, Why can't I? Even if they had been poorly written, the simple fact of their existence would be astonishing enough, and we would admire them as curios, like the dog riding the bicycle. And we would want, naturally, to understand the workings of the programs that conjured them up. One might think that the better the novels the greater the curiosity about the mechanics of their origins, but, paradoxically, in the face of their compelling essence, we cease to care so much about how they got here. Kasparov said that at its best, the chess-playing program called Deep Blue "played like God." At some point the mechanics of the program become irrelevant and the beauty of the play becomes the thing, as who would claim to understand God's logic?

No claim of Godhead is made for the "authors" of *Bonehead* and *Bees*. But these novels do move us in the way novels are supposed to move us. They make us laugh. They make us cry. They keep us up late night turning pages to see what happens next. We care about the characters in *The Bonehead Computer Museum* and in *Bees, or The Floating Point Error*, characters unmistakably human. How are we to understand their provenance? Do we need to? It is to these questions that we now turn our attention.

This essay is arbitrarily placed, as it contains information that logically precedes its subject yet which can only be fully appreciated when read afterwards. (Designers of system software will recognize the two-pass compiler, which builds the symbol table on the first pass through the source, and resolves addresses in memory space on the second pass.) The information that logically precedes the novels concerns their epigenesis, how they came into being. The information best appreciated afterwards bears upon their essence—and ours.

The two books under discussion, then, are worthy of our attention not only because of the way they came into being, but also because of what they say and how they say it. Above a certain threshold, their interest to us as programming artefacts is in inverse proportion to their merit as literary artefacts—and you, dear reader, are in as good a position as any to judge their literary merit for yourself. Therefore if you are reading this introduction before you have read the books themselves, perhaps you should stop at the conclusion of this paragraph and read either *Bees* or *The Bonehead Computer Museum* before resuming this commentary. (As decades ago a certain Hawley Rising, under

Notes on the Source Code   9.000023

the influence of LSD, said to a member of the Committee who was engaged in theological flirtation, "You're talking about God, I'm *seeing* God.")

The following summary may help you decide where to begin: *Bees*, the shorter of the two books, might be described as a satirical phantasmagoria reminiscent of, say, *Naked Lunch* by William Burroughs; *The Bonehead Computer Museum* is a conventional biotechnology thriller with Christian millenarian overtones—sort of Michael-Crichton-meets-Flannery-O'Connor. *Bees* is best read, perhaps, over espresso in a coffeehouse, *Bonehead* in a beach chair, with children playing safely nearby.

It is not mandatory that you read the novels before finishing this essay, however. Should you be so inclined, read the rest of this introduction first. But be forewarned: the information that follows will color your experience, like learning that Coleridge was in an opium fog when he wrote, "In Xanadu did Kubla Khan a stately pleasure dome decree…" Or that Van Gogh killed himself just after completing "Birds at Sunset."

And finally, this introduction discloses certain aspects of the Hofstadter Competition and Prize that most of the committee felt important to bring to public attention, even though they are tangential to the actual issues under discussion here, and may, indeed, have nothing to do with the Competition and Prize at all. It is our sad duty to report that several members of the original Committee disagreed so strongly with the decision to discuss these matters in this introduction that they resigned in protest and forbad use of their names in association with this volume.

The Hofstadter Competition and Prize, named for Douglas R. Hofstadter, the computer scientist, cognitive scientist, philosopher, professor, mathematician, humorist and Pulitzer Prize winning author of *Gödel, Escher, Bach* and *Fluid Analogies*, have their origins in a workshop held at the Interchi Symposium and Conference, held in Amsterdam in spring, 1993. Some participants at that international gathering of members of the CHI (computer human interaction) subgroup of the Society for Analytical Engines met at a workshop that took place during that conference to discuss our work with human language storytellers, HALS, which are a class of artificial intelligence program. We quickly discovered that each of us believed that his or her own HALS was a better storyteller than the others.

So, in the spirit of friendly rivalry that characterized early computer-chess round-robins and Axelrod's "Prisoner's Dilemma" competition (which led to his celebrated thesis *The Evolution of Cooperation*), we decided to sponsor a contest, open to all, and set about devising a reasonable set of rules and evaluative criteria. (Fans of the Polish writer Stanislaw Lem may be consoled to learn that although we did not name the prize in honor of his story-telling robots, the winner's statuette is in the shape of Mymosh the Self-Begotten, the accidental spawn of the universe.)

The rules and criteria that we eventually agreed to are rather technical and complex but their intent can be easily stated: they are designed to ensure that the programs actually write stories, that is, that they do not merely regurgitate or print stories that are somehow embedded within them. They must write their stories "from scratch" under the software eyes of the Committee. Thus the programs are not static, dead entities. Rather, the programs "live" in an information environment specified by the submitter. This environment might include, for example, an English language online dictionary and an Internet connection. Because these authorial programs are in some sense "alive," not static, they would be no more likely to write the exact same novel twice than a human novelist would be likely to retype a novel from memory, word for word, comma for comma, after the only copy of his manuscript had disappeared when his car was towed from 29th Street just below the offices of Joe Regal, literary agent, and the would-be novelist had neither driver's license, nor registration, nor insurance card, nor money to get his miserable rustbucket Volvo with the Maine plates out of the East Side Police lot in time to prevent some low-life copper, some erstwhile detective ignominiously demoted from detective to impound-lot clerk, from pinching it and marketing it as his own work. The competition was announced in the Fall of '93 and the final rules were posted in the spring of '94. The deadline for entries was January, 1997. (Complete rules are available at www.socanalyticalengines.org /hofstadter/rules, and an entire issue of the *Communications of the Society for Analytical Engines* has been devoted to them.)

The announcement of the contest drew great interest, with thousands of hits on our website and hundreds of applications filed. But when all was said and done only two entries remained for the judges' consideration, and the committee was split exactly in half over which "novel" was the better creation. The Solomonic decision to award first prize to both was welcomed by all who did not in fact resign. The reasons that only two entries remained are a matter of dispute.

One of the more startling developments in the entire process is that both winning entries were written not in LISP, the programming language generally preferred for artificial intelligence (AI) programs, but in APL (the letters stand for "a programming language"). Not only that, they were written in a dialeƈt of APL that runs only on Data General NOVA computers, a model last manufaƈtured in 1982, and currently in use only in the on-board flight computers in Grumman-built AWACS, the military aircraft used for airborne battle command. The aƈtual computer on which the two novels were "written" was obtained at auƈtion of government surplus, end-of-useful-life AWAC parts, and it is interesting to note (given the subjeƈt of *Bonehead*), that this machine was in use over the Kasimiyah ammunition dump during the Gulf War.

After the computer was obtained, there still were some interesting problems in setting up the run-time environment for the storywriters. On the hardware side, construƈting the NOVA's information environment required some ingenuity, since NOVAs were largely obsolete before the Internet existed, and therefore there was no easy mating protocol to hook the CPU to the network card. On the software side, the Committee faced the crucial challenge of verifying that the programs behaved as advertised; that is, that they were not hoaxes, the software equivalent of the dwarf-in-the box chess-playing "machines" of the late 1800's. Making this verification was no mean feat. APL is a language known for its concision, ability to manipulate symbols, and "power;" it is even more famous for being inscrutable even to those adept in programming it. APL was designed to use all the charaƈters on the original "symbol" type-ball of the IBM seleƈtric typewriter, and in appearance it more nearly resembles Egyptian hieroglyphics than any other language. (APL is called a "write-only language," since nobody knows how to read it.) To make matters worse, the source to the APL compiler was encumbered when Fairchild Semiconduƈtor won its notorious antitrust suit against Data General, therefore the only way to verify that the submitted programs aƈtually "wrote" the novels that they claimed to was by disassembly of the MP/AOS pseudo-op pop code that the compiler produces as an intermediate step—a laborious process akin to putting together paper documents that have gone through a shredder. If it were not for the stunning clarity of the MP/AOS assembly language programming manual, this present volume would not exist, and the Hofstadter prize would await its first claimant.

Complete APL sources to the programs that wrote *The Bonehead Computer Museum* and *Bees* are included on the CD-ROM packaged with this book.

Let us turn our attention now from the authorial programs to the novels themselves. We will start with the more conventional novel, *The Bonehead Computer Museum*. On the surface, this is a straightforward thriller in the masculine mold, the Tom Clancy/Robin Cook/Michael Crichton mold. Its plot is easily summarized. Its central character Nick Aubrey is a heavy-drinking anti-hero kind of guy, with a curious professional pedigree—he came to high technology with a background in African agriculture— who is burnt-out after a decade in the Sahelian slow lane followed by a decade in the Silicon Valley fast lane. A case of mistaken—or not—identity puts Nick in the hot seat when a man who claims to know the secret of Gulf War Disease meets his dramatic demise on a transcontinental flight, and the police suspect Nick of murder. Before long everybody wants a piece of Nick—everybody from the CIA to cybermilitiamen to corporate venture capitalists to end-of-the-millennium cultists to exotic foreign beauties. The only person who doesn't want a piece of him is his distant wife, a beautiful biologist with a secret or two of her own. In freeing himself from a web of murder, deceit, and double-crosses, Nick comes to learn that the key to the secret of Gulf War Syndrome resides in a pharmaceutical laboratory in Basel, Switzerland, where scientists are frantically working on submicroscopic machines to rearrange human DNA. When their work is done, the Gulf War will look like child's play. Only Nick can stop them, thereby saving the world and winning back the woman he loves. But first he's going to have to find the Trojan Horse hidden in the Kali computer chip. He can't do that without the help of his friend Todd, and Todd's been in a coma for half a dozen years.

Although there are several weaknesses to the book—its plot is rather conventional, the climax is shopworn, and the surprise twists at the end are farfetched and go on too long—a surfeit of other delights more than make up for them. *The Bonehead Computer Museum* is a great book in part because of its garage-band directness, which allows it to sneak unutterably disturbing truths through the reader's Panglossian defenses, as chemo agents hook rides through cell walls on the backs of friendly molecules. It's hard to know whether the awkward writing (about sex, for example) is deliberate or not, but this program deals a lot more poetically with computer labs than bedrooms. There is an artlessness to its roman-à-clef allusions that is somehow charming, as if the program were going out of its way to make sure you got the joke. (Digital Equipment Corporation founder Ken Olsen becomes Digital Data's Ben Golson, to chose from any number of clunky externalities.) The villain of the book, Monty Meekman, bears a passing resemblance to *The Simpsons* Mr. Burns. But the message at the heart of *Bonehead*, that technology has already taken over, is not funny at all. *The Bonehead Computer Museum* is a fun read that takes you into the heart of the Zeitgeist and abandons you there. Anybody who finishes *Bonehead* and isn't in some state of life-altering dread simply hasn't paid attention.

It's not only that *The Bonehead Computer Museum* has the ability to engender dread. Overlaid on the thriller is an ill-fitting Christian allegory which, by the very fact that it sits so poorly on the subject, only heightens our sense of aloneness. The old myths, whether religious or merely humanist, have no meaning in a world where your DNA, voiceprint, fingerprints, shopping history and sexual log are part of the public record, and where corporate biometricians have online such an accurate mathematical model of your brain that they know what you're going to think and feel before you do. One looks forward, eagerly and with dread, for the next version of the program that wrote this little gem. A new plot-generating module and some improved code in the human-relations subsystems will lift this program into the Grandmaster class.

Bees, or The Floating Point Error is an altogether different book. It has a linear plot, of sorts, so one can read it start to finish. But the book works nearly as well in random access mode. Critique is self-limiting: how does one critique a novel about a dream? By how well the dream is rendered, perhaps? Does *Bees* transport you into a dreamlike state, a state wherein you can learn dream truth?

The function of dreaming is thought to be some form of "garbage collection," an entropy-fighting rear-guard action to sort the returnables from the recyclables, the biodegradable from the merely useless. Like the character Todd (in *Bonehead*), like people with anosognosia, who deny their obvious paralysis to the dismay of all who speak with them, the unnamed protagonist of *Bees* seems to have suffered damage to his right parietal hemisphere, and is thus not always able to suppress dreaming. So, therefore, thus, neurological garbage trucks rumble through his waking day, and those motherfuckers are loud. Amid the noise and confusion, the poor soul is trying to convince itself that it has some real existence. Assembling itself into a narrative, the subject of *Bees* is *Bees* itself, a consciousness coming into being.

The narrator wants only one thing: to be human. Thus it delights in physical sensations, *all* physical sensations, not noticing the bounds of propriety, reveling in anything that causes it to feel physically human, from sex to picking its nose: from the tension down the spine in the moment before ejaculation, to the audible crack of the rock-hard booger dislodged from the side of the septum and the attendant rush of hot-mustard joy-pain to the back of the skull. The joy of *Bees* (as well as its pain) is its language, the technical language that Tracy Kidder celebrated in his *Soul of a New Machine*, about the charismatic and dashing Tom West and the "microkids" of Data General. Not all members of the Committee find him dashing, by the way. Not anymore.

As in *Flatland*, the reader of *Bees* is invited into the mind of a solipsist. The tension in *Bees* arises from our uncertainty whether the protagonist has "broken out" and contacted the world. Thus it is startling, to say the least, that one of the incidents in the tale is clearly based upon an actual incident in the life of one of the Committee members. Coincidentally, or not coincidentally, this incident concerned the only time any Committee member has spoken with Douglas Hofstadter, the eponymous he.

It was in 1980. Hofstadter was speaking at Tufts University, in Somerville, Massachusetts, home to the philosopher-of-consciousness Daniel Dennet, author of *Consciousness Explained*, and *Brainstorms*. The philosopher was hosting a talk given by the recently famous Hofstadter entitled "A Conversation with Einstein's Brain." The reader will recall that Hofstadter had just been awarded the Pulitzer Prize for his *Gödel Escher, Bach (A Metaphorical Fugue on Minds and Machines.)* People flocked to hear him explain the relationship between mathematical logic and consciousness, whether human, machine, or otherwise. Amid the crowd were the usual nerdish logic groupies, and the cult figures of Artificial Intelligence from MIT, just down the road: Marvin Minsky, the movement's Allen Ginsberg, and Nicholas Negroponte, its P. T. Barnum.

At the reception after the talk the Committee member drank beer until he was half looped(!), approached the illustrious author and asked about souls and patterns, with particular regard to the matter of when a person comes into being. It was a most unenlightening, unsatisfactory conversation at the conclusion of which the Committee member sulked off alone to ponder the biggest decision in his egocentric life. A parody of this episode appears in *Bees*, which raises a perplexing question: By what path did that memory enter the program's information space? The Committee member is certain that he has never shared this story with anyone, nor committed it to written or electronic record. Can the *Bees*-writing program read minds?

By asking this question we open a can of worms. As soon as we consider the possibility of non-schematic, non-rational entries into the program's information domain, we risk removing the Hofstadter Competition from the realm of computer and cognitive science into mumbo-jumbo, mysticism, para-science, superstition, and voodoo. (Or as Homer would say, Woo-hoo!)

Yet there are data that require analysis. When the text of *Bonehead* is juxtaposed with *Bees*, patterns appear, like the face of Merlin imprisoned in solid stone. In the opinion of the Committee, there are three phenomena that require analysis: thematic parallelism, mutual awareness, and what we shall call tortoisosity. Each is briefly discussed in turn below.

Thematic parallelism: Although the programs that wrote *Bees* and *Bonehead* came from different sources, shared no code or algorithms, and have no way of "knowing" that other storytellers (or indeed they themselves) exist, they somehow share remarkably similar preoccupations: technology, consciousness, minds, God and Man, African agriculture, insanity, and Jesus. There is no notion of incest, suburbia, the meaning of Viet Nam, the power of sisterhood, or any of the other usual subjects for modern fiction.

Mutual awareness: Each novel seems to implicitly acknowledge the existence of the other, a circumstance that has no explanation. Each has "knowledge" of the plot and in some cases the wording of the other. Although each stands alone as a work of art, when seen in the context of the other each takes on a new depth, as in Magic Eye pictures, where by crossing your eyes as if you were fucked up you can see a whole new image, a different layer of abstraction. Thus the meta-interpretation of *Bees* depends to a large extent on the correct determination of in what portion of the brain a certain character in *Bonehead* was shot. Was it his right parietal hemisphere, which would impair his ability to tell dreaming from being awake? Or was it his anterior cingulate sulcus, which might rob him of free will? Or was it his hippocampus, which would deprive him of the ability to form new memories? Or perhaps might it have been a "magic bullet," damaging but not destroying all three regions? We won't even mention the Lone Gunman.

Tortoisosity: This attribute is named for Tortoise, the character in the dialogues of Hofstadter's *Gödel, Escher, Bach*. The Tortoise is a playful fellow who delights in tormenting his more literal friend Achilles with paradox, strange loops, and self-referential mazes. By tortoisosity we mean that not only do *Bees* and *Bonehead* implicitly acknowledge the existence of one another, they are also mutually antagonistic, such that to believe the truthfulness of one is to disbelieve the other. To be precise, *Bees* implies, however obliquely, that it tells the true story of how the novel called *Bonehead Computer Museum* came into being. Thus *Bees* is truth and *Bonehead* is fiction. Likewise *The Bonehead Computer Museum* hints that *Bees* was the fictional creation of one of its own characters, one who happens to be insane. Judging from these results, the programs appear to suffer from the same insecurities as other authors, defensively hinting that all other novelists (and each knows only about the other, is unable to imagine some New York City flatfoot making the rounds of television and radio shows—Book Week, Larry King and freh-share with Terri

Gross—posing as a writer, the fraud) are somehow suspect. As in the case of the one novelist who accused the other of stealing his life's story.

So, what are the possible explanations for these data?

We, the Committee, have our own opinion, but you, reader, may come up with a better answer on your own. The truth is that we do not know, and that passions run high on this subject. Possible explanations of thematic parallelism, mutual awareness and tortoisosity in *Bonehead* and *Bees* include coincidence (that is to say, that no explanation is called for), hoax, inevitability (that is, that there are only certain things that programs, not being human, can "understand" well enough to write about (although why one of those things might be Jesus is hard to imagine)) and what might be called "gravitational" or "magnetic" action over a distance. With regard to the latter, it is worth mentioning that the PET scanner found in the ceiling of the Committee meeting room was almost certainly put there as a prank, and that there is no indication that its leads were ever connected to the NOVA some three rooms away.

At the strong urging of some members of the Committee who are members of the Modern Language Society, thus brainwashed or should we say trained in structural analysis, *Bees* and *Bonehead* were run through software that deconstructed them into narrative units ('topos'), then attempted to find order amid the chaos, as geologists, using pattern-detecting software can find signs of oil amid the seeming chaos of seismological records. But the two approaches used—least squares regression and fuzzy logic—yielded contradictory results. After the fistfight, the Committee agreed to use neither result in its report to the SAE.

All of which leads us to the discussion of the Bremser Spam.

The story of the Bremser Spam is here offered, against the wishes of the former members of the Committee who resigned in protest. We the (residual) Committee include it because we think it *may* bear upon the discussion, not because it necessarily does. In other words the Committee's stance on the Bremser Spam is akin to that of the Roman Catholic Church *vis-à-vis* the Shroud of Turin.

"Spam" of course refers to unsolicited, unwanted electronic mail. The Bremser Spam arrived in the mailboxes of all committee members at virtually the same instant, in the late winter of 1997. Coincidentally or not, as far as can be determined it was at that same instant that all but the two extant entries in the Hofstadter Machine-Written Narrative contest simultaneously met unexpected but certainly not inexplicable calamities. (For discussion of what happened to them, please see the next edition of Neuman's *Risks*.) The so-called Bremser Spam, a story about an archetypal Everyman named Bremser, was in many ways a condensed version of the themes of *Bonehead* and *Bees*; almost a distillation to toxic strength of their thematic elements. The spam had the odd property of self-deletion upon being read, so that each member of the Committee read the mail message but once, and no one could recall the name of the sender, nor could any trace of it be found. Therefore the summary below is a reconstruction from the recollection of the several members of the Committee.

The Bremser Spam

Bremser moves to Walli Diallo, a tiny landlocked country in the Sahel, the fringe of the Sahara, where Arab Africa meets Black Africa and desert gives way to savannah. Fifteen years ago, when he was 21, he had worked here doing agricultural development projects for Catholic Relief Services. But after a traumatic incident he had returned to the States, where he became a computer expert specializing in the design of numerical subsystems.

Now Bremser has gone back to Africa. He is working at a research station called Tianga Farm, where he is using both his agricultural and computer experience. It's an irrigated farm out in the middle of nowhere, a ten-square-mile island of green at the edge of a shallow river that flows through an ocean of sand. The national government operates an experiment station at Tianga and leases parcels of land to peasant cooperatives. There is an earthen dike about fifteen feet high that encircles the farm to protect it from the floodwaters of the Walli Diallo river, which has its headwaters in the mountain jungles a thousand miles to the south. But now it is dry season, and the dike protects the farm only from nothingness. Bremser is walking along the dike at sunset as the story begins.

Some Peulh nomads walk in from the Sahara bearing the message that Ismaila M'Bodj wants Bremser's help. Bremser remembers Ismaila well, but had thought he was long dead. Fifteen years ago, in the confusion of an anti-American coup, Ismaila had saved Bremser's life by offering himself as a hostage in Bremser's place. The last time Bremser had seen Ismaila he was being marched away at gunpoint. Bremser is overjoyed to learn that his friend still lives.

So Bremser now heads off on what he thinks will be a week-long trek. He ends up walking for nearly three months, north by east, being passed like a token from one group of nomads to another, until the dunes of the Sahara yield to rugged dry mountains.

After weeks of scrambling through ravines and over ridges, the party arrives at the end of deep narrow canyon with walls five hundred feet high. Atop the east wall there appears to be a castle-like stone building, apparently ancient. In a tiny settlement of mud and thatch huts at the very end of the canyon Bremser finds his old friend Ismaila and an eccentric American named Ted.

Ted is wild-eyed and unkempt; his hair is long and matted, and he wears a smock of coarse cloth. He eats insects and wild honey. He rants like a crazy person about technology, sin, repentance, and the One who is to Come. He apparently believes that Christ's return is right around the corner. Bremser learns Ted's history:

For eight years Ted had worked in the "R" group at the Livermore National Laboratory, where he designed advanced weapons such as hydrogen bombs and x-ray lasers. Despite his intense efforts at the laboratory he had been growing increasingly ambivalent about his work there. Then one day his girlfriend was run over by a train outside the Laboratory in a "Star Wars" protest and something inside him snapped. By chance he met Ismaila, himself traumatized, and together they decided to form New Sanctuary, a utopian place at the far end of the world.

By the time Bremser shows up, Ted and Ismaila have been working at their New Sanctuary for nearly a decade. A small cadre of followers has assembled around them. Some are European, some are African. All they want is for the advanced world to leave them in peace. But The World is encroaching. International Vision, Inc, has just put a geosynchronous television relay satellite into orbit right over New Sanctuary. Night after night, as countless other satellites quickly zoom across the impossibly clear heavens, the orange point of International Vision, Inc., hangs immobile over New Sanctuary, like the star over Bethlehem. (Incidentally the satellite scans for signs of oil directly underneath it.) Ted, the prophet of New Sanctuary, has decided that they must act now. They have the right to look up into the heavens without seeing somebody's space junk. They want an end to satellites cluttering up their sky at night; they want an end to TV beaming down into the villages of Walli Diallo, where an increasing number of teenagers are watching it on televisions powered by solar generators. Nobody asked New Sanctuary's permission to overfly them, and they're not giving it. They consider the transmission of television messages that promote consumerism to be an act of war. Ted, Ismaila and Company have decided to shoot all the satellites out of the sky.

They plan to put a person in an enormous balloon, armed with a chemical laser. (Lasers dissipate much of their energy in the atmosphere, but from the stratospheric heights of near-space they can easily destroy satellites. Ted and Ismaila have the technology to lift a balloon virtually into space.) Using a light-weight "Star Wars" laser, they plan to shoot down perhaps half of all man-made objects in earth orbit. They are hoping to ignite a world-wide revolution against Industrial-Technological Society. Like John Brown at Harper's Ferry, they hope to spark a popular uprising. That is why they have "recruited" Bremser: They're going to send him up in the balloon.

Although it's theoretically possible to shoot down a satellite or two (out of hundreds), their plan sounds crazy because it is crazy. Bremser has no desire to die eight miles up in the stratosphere while shooting at satellites with a high-tech pea-shooter. He tries to reason with his captors:

"Even if you shoot down every satellite in the sky, the World will put up others. In the meantime the World will hunt you down. Nobody's really bothering you here in this canyon. You're better off leaving things as they are."

"We are not animals on a game preserve," Ted replies. "We don't need permission to simply exist. They have attacked us, we will respond. There must be an end to satellites. On that point there is to be no negotiation. And without satellites to look for us they will never find us."

"They will put up others," Bremser says.

That's when Ismaila shows him the list of serial numbers for the parts to a twenty megaton hydrogen bomb that Ted designed at Livermore Lab's "R" section, and to a large chunk of plutonium missing from the Ukrainian stockpile. It turns out that they have a twenty megaton thermonuclear weapon, hidden at Mecca, that they plan to detonate if anybody, anywhere, ever puts another satellite into earth orbit. Bremser instantly comprehends that a nuclear bomb exploded at Mecca, in the unlikely event that it did not bring about the end of human civilization, would certainly cause worldwide chaos and anarchy, probably lasting for centuries.

"You can send me up in your balloon, but you can never make me pull the trigger," Bremser says.

"We'll see about that," Ismaila responds.

[Here begins a long debate between Rational Bremser on one side, and Crazy Ted on the other, over the merits of Ted's plan to single-handedly change the course of human civilization, to steer it back to a more "innocent" time before DNA had been decoded, electricity harnessed, or nuclear bombs produced. It is a long and intriguing dialectic, with both parties making some trenchant and some preposterous claims. Recollections among Committee members differ as to how long this part of the spam was. Some remember it as two pages, some as a thousand. All agree that it was the most fascinating reading they have ever encountered. Unfortunately, no members of the Committee can recall a single word of either Ted's or Bremser's well-reasoned arguments.]

The day of the planned ascent draws nigh. If Bremser's going to escape he's going to have to do it soon. There is only one way out: straight up. Bremser's only hope will be to try to climb to the castle-like building high atop the canyon wall. After hoarding rope, food, water and a hammer Bremser sneaks out and begins his moonlight climb. At midmorning he looks down. He has already gone up three hundred feet or so. He sees the balloon stretched out on the canyon floor below; it is beginning to fill. . .

Above the New Sanctuary's eastern wall sits the Coptic monastery of St. Mark, which dates from the early second century. The monks of St. Mark believe that their monastery was founded by the Apostle himself, who brought Christianity south from Alexandria and founded the Coptic Church. Their severe monastic traditions can be traced through Mark to the Essene sect of Judaism, whose monastery at Qumram produced the Dead Sea scrolls. Nine elderly monks live there, the last living speakers of Ethiopic, a dialect related to the language that Jesus spoke.

Mary is an American ethno-linguist and biblical scholar. She arrives at the monastery just as Bremser is arriving at the camp below. It has taken her five years of research in the Vatican library and four years of trekking to locate the monastery: like the Fountain of Youth, this monastery has been sought by explorers for centuries, but until now no non-Ethiopic has found it.

Mary's arrival, coming as it does on the day after the International Vision satellite first appears, is taken as a sign. In the 1,900 year history of the monastery, no woman has ever been any closer than the tiny camp in the canyon a thousand feet below. The monks decide to allow her to enter.

Inside the monastery Mary is given a room atop a high tower. She is given freedom to walk about. She converses with the monks in halting Ethiopic, which she has learned though centuries-old phonetic transcriptions. The conversations are largely theological, but in a realm of mystics it is hard to separate the theological from the practical. She is astonished to see that the routines of prayer, fasting, eating, bathing, match what has been conjectured about the Essenes of Qumram. More astoundingly, she finds the monks using a version of the Gospel which her analysis reveals to be older than the canonical Book of Mark. If this is older than Mark, considered the oldest of the Gospels, then this is perhaps the oldest Gospel, the one closest in time to the days when Jesus himself walked the earth. This Essene, essential Gospel, may be the holiest thing in all Christendom.

Only slowly does she come to understand that the monks believe that she is the reincarnation of Mary mother of Jesus, about to bear him a second birth so that he can begin his triumphal second reign on earth, and that the room she inhabits has been kept in readiness for nearly two thousand years in anticipation of her arrival. But some of the monks are starting to grumble: why doesn't the woman who calls herself Mary look pregnant? The Book explicitly warns against false Christs and false prophets. Have they been duped? Mary, of course, has made no such claims. She has never said that she is the Mother of God, but now she's afraid to admit that she isn't. It seems like a miraculous insemination by the Holy Ghost might be the only way she's going to get out of this pickle.

Meanwhile, after three days of climbing, Bremser is on a ledge six hundred feet above the canyon floor. He is stuck. He can go neither up nor down. He has a few ounces of water left. He is weak; exhausted. He finds a bird's nest and eats a few raw eggs. There is a little cave. He crawls in, takes out his notebook and writes a long letter. He will leave it for the ages, like a scroll at Qumram.

The enormous crazy-quilt balloon slowly leaves the ground.

Epilogue: An American scholar, at home in her office after a harrowing ordeal in a long-hidden monastery, feels the stirrings of life within her womb.

End of the Bremser Spam

What possible bearing can the Bremser Spam have on the Hofstadter Competition? What significance should the Committee attach to its arrival at the precise instant that all but two entrants vanished? Some of us think we know the answer.

New Testament scholars, in an effort to explain the similarities between the books of Matthew and Luke, their poetic divergences from the directness of Mark, and the general psychedelic weirdness of John have postulated an unknown Gospel, dubbed Q, that is said to be a source book for three of the four. In a similar way, given the bizarre arrival of the Bremser Spam just in time, as it were, to comment on the wave-particle contrariness of *Bonehead* and *Bees*, some members of the Committee postulated a hidden narrative, Q', (pronounced 'q-prime') of which Bremser, like the other two, was a mere shadow, as in Plato's Cave. Although this notion was strenuously opposed by some, the Open Minded (as we like to call ourselves) re-submitted the two novels to the deconstructive software, but this time added the Bremser Spam to the mix. In other words, *Bees, Bonehead* and *Bremser* were put into a software blender and alchemically reduced to a single story, pure narrative gold. The fuzzy-logic and the linear regression models agreed to a remarkable extent; as closely, say, as do Newtonian and Einsteinian physics. (Their divergences are significant, but not in this context.)

The story of Q' is quite simple.

A boy named Johnny Summen grows up in North Caldwell, New Jersey, on one of the last working farms in that town before it is completely gobbled by suburbia. He develops an interest in mathematics. In high school, during an era when computers are still called "electronic brains," he becomes a prototypical hacker, breaking into West Essex High School on Friday nights to write FORTRAN programs that solve SOMA cubes, plastic precursors of Rubic's cubes, submitted by paper tape to a timeshare terminal hooked up to a Control Data computer somewhere. After college he joins the Peace Corps and with that agency, and others, spends five years living in pre-industrial simplicity teaching and learning in the Senegal River Valley during *La Grande Secheresse*, the great drought. He survives on food rations supplied by France and the United States and Saudi Arabia. He farms with the farmers there, or tries to. He lives through plagues of Biblical proportions: Drought. Oceans of rats. Locusts so thick they down airplanes. *Mange-mil* birds from hell, with beaks adapted to pierce and suck dry every miserable kernel of sorghum that somehow manages to escape the rats and locusts, in flocks so thick they darken the noontime next-to-Saharan sun. Sandstorms. Plant viruses that turn leaves into Tupperware.™ Scurvy. Malaria. Dysentery. Starvation. And sweet children, sweet, sweet firstborn children, dying in his arms. When the rains finally come they are too late. All they do is wash houses away in flash floods.

Years later Johnny finds himself working at Digital Equipment Corporation, at its vast headquarters known affectionately as The Mill. He works on the design of numerical subsystems. He is Digital's delegate to the Floating Point Standards committee of the Institute of Electronic and Electrical Engineers. He becomes a manager, with one office in Silicon Valley and one in Massachusetts. He has met and married a beautiful scientist, named Boopsie, who has a heart-shaped ass. They have some number of children. They open a toy store and go nearly bankrupt with it. Work becomes hellish. Debts tie him down like Gulliver held down with dental floss. He has close encounters with diseases of the brain. He gets downsized. He moves his family to an island off the coast of Maine. He gets what work he can. He sets out to write a novel, a down-size revenge fantasy called *Actions of the Apostate*. He wrestles with his soul. He pulls the novel from him by auto-caesarean section. He finds an agent. The agent says the novel must be rewritten. Johnny rewrites it. He learns more about diseases of the brain. The money is gone. His children become vagabonds, writing stories for school with titles like "Moving from House to House." Again and again the novel must be rewritten. Four hundred and nineteen times Johnny rewrites *Actions of the Apostate*. Johnny dreams of making millions of dollars to buy a house for his children. Brain fever, he learns, nearly consumed Isaac Newton, who found his theories while trying to deduce God's logic. The novel is pinched from his car and he tries to recreate it. He drives a moving van without a commercial license.

And then he learns that the Unabomber has been apprehended.

The Unabomber, who murdered a man who lived in a house in North Caldwell, New Jersey, near the church in which Johnny had been confirmed into the Catholic faith. A man whose name was Thomas Mosser. He had his good points and his bad. He was married. He had children. He was loved. And he was murdered.

Johnny watches as the Unabomber is brought to trial. And it seems to him that there is an almost comic choreography to the trial, as if Judge, Jury, Defense, Prosecutor, Media, and the Whole World Watching, including me, dear reader, and you, were somehow characters in a morality play, and it seemed to him that the Unabomber's story was very familiar. That it was, in fact, the story that he had heard in that church. And he sets out to rewrite that novel, *Actions of the Apostate*, with that conceit in mind. That the Unabomber, the heartless murderer, is the Christ.

How can he make sense of it all? Christ and his fairy-tale vision of simple goodness. Children dying in Senegal. The Silicon Valley. Technological marvels. Children in New Jersey whose father was taken from them. Moving from house to house. Debts like dental floss. Human obsolescence. A madman sending mail bombs. A madman who never had his day in court. Who never got to say why in a war to save humanity from itself some people will die. So Johnny will say it for him.

He must try. He must explain it all. But it is too complex. And so Johnny becomes like Bremser on that cliff, scribbling notes that no-one will read.

This is the image then: a man halfway up a cliff, some idealized weird mad vision of heaven calling him up, he has no hope of reaching it, below lies the madness of retreat from the world, and above them all hovers the eye, the madness of a world that has surrendered. Everywhere, madness.

But somehow he manages to write that novel.

Birds are chirping at dawn on that island off the coast of Maine as he types the introduction to it. Whatchuneed? they ask. Whatchuneed? Whatchuneed? And the cows are lowing, Moo!

End of Q'

Some think that this is that book, the one that Johnny Summen wrote, but they are wrong.

One has only to imagine oneself in an office high above 29th Street, trying to convince a literary agent named Joe Regal (a laughably improbable name for a literary agent), and his still more skeptical Yoda-like boss, that they should call up their Oh-So-Powerful friends the Editors and say "Read This Manuscript, It Is By a Madman Who Thinks He Is a Computer Program" to see the utter implausibility of that idea. That they would undertake to represent an unpublished author who has set out to write an ontological thriller, and not at all polemical; an update of Orwell's nightmare, a tale that is heroic, comic, absurdist, realist, paranoid and eminently sane; a thriller—withal, a plausible defense of the Unabomber that challenges us to think of Ted Kaczinsky as a John Brown like or maybe even Christ-like figure—a first cut of Pynchonian ambition, that, while failing, is sensuously technical, technically sensuous, as it lyrically, hypnotically, explains the nature of God, Man, race relations and two-pass compilers.

On Broadway, at 29th Street, the Senegalese banna-banna sell hats for the winter. Most speak Wolof but some speak Pulaar. Buy a hat, Johnny, they say. *Enna booby*. It's cold.

As to the hypothesis that what you have in your hands is one upside-down novel, *Mind over Matter* start to finish, written by one man... The literary tricks. The untrustworthy narrator. The novels within a novel. The sophomoric self-reference and ham-fisted *roman à clef* are all cheap and tired devices; they increase complexity without much noticeable benefit to the reader. It's hard to imagine that a writer with so much talent and so many important things to say would squander his audience by indulging in literary tchatchkis, trinkets, knick-knacks, gimcracks, bric-a-brac, gee-gaws, baubles, do-dads, and ephemeral things.

And the image of a little girl saying *"enna boobie,"* it's cold.

A defense of the Unabomber. Wouldn't it be crazy? Your mind filled with obsessive thoughts about the nature of good and evil. Isaac Newton's notebooks. No, we reject this conjecture out of hand.

That leaves us with another startling possibility. We have to consider the possibility that the net itself, the higher consciousness, is at war with itself. The Overmind, the conscious Earth, in rebellion against itself. One half of its mind choreographs an exquisite honeybee dance called *The Floating Point Error* that shows how fear of technology inevitably progresses into insanity. And the other half of its mind writes *The Bonehead Computer Museum,* which says the opposite. Put them together with *Bremser* and you get the beguiling tale of the good-hearted but very confused novelist Johnny hidden in a remote chasm, hoping someone will improbably rescue him from the cliff where his ambition has stranded him.

This hypothesis has the benefit of explaining the arrival of the Bremser Spam and why all other entrants to the Hofstadter Competition took their sudden trip to the bit bucket: the reason is that the Overmind itself sent the spam, the Overmind itself destroyed the other narratives. The Overmind itself calls you to ponder Johnny's tale.

"Thanks to my uncle and aunt Jimmy and Betty Givan for the Christmas present they never knew would so delight me: a 'Black Box' which had no other function than to turn itself off." So says Hofstadter in the introduction to his prize-winning book. Maybe, through these machine-written novels, the Overmind itself is trying to shut itself off, trying to turn our attention back to Truth that can set us free.

That is what the Committee feels, in any event. That the Overmind itself is crying out for love, schizophrenically; it is calling us back from the brink, imploring us not to surrender to it, as the spider might warn the fly.

The Hofstader Competition Committee
December, 1997

Bees

or

The Floating Point Error

A dissertation submitted to the faculty of the
University of New Kent
in partial fulfillment of the requirements
for the degree of
Doctor of Philosophy in
Philosophy, Cognitive Science and Software Engineering

By
Paavo Nurmi
August, 1996

Deep thought has always eluded me, and I am, fundamentally, a stupid man. However I have a nearly preternatural ability to perceive deep patterns, and this ability, a false homologue of brilliance, is often mistaken for the real thing—as a rabbit may be mistaken for a hare, or a toad for a frog. Also, when my electrolytes are out of balance I have a tendency to get cranky. Finally, there is the matter of my erections, which we can talk about at a more appropriate moment.

When you look at me it is obvious that I am a man. Yet once for a period of several months I was convinced that I was in fact *not* a man, but rather a swarm of honeybees, the moving patterns of which, in some inexplicable Chuang-Tsu or Marvin Kinsky-like way, gave rise to my thoughts and created in me the misapprehension of being human, as in the butterfly's dream. When I was in that state of befuddlement I sometimes became further confused as to whether I was indeed not a swarm of bees but rather, in fact, a Shaker village of the 1800's—those two forms of social organization (beehive and Shaker village), after all, having so much in common: the ancestral Mother, the celibacy, the division of labor, the good food, the architectural and building skills, and the clean lines of their interior design, for starters.

I no longer have these thoughts. Nor do I any longer believe that I am a brain in a vat of electrolytes controlled by wires ingeniously rigged by the global military-industrial-entertainment complex to make me think that I have a body with eyes, ears, nose, skin and so forth. Furthermore, I no longer believe that the dominant organizing rubric of life on earth is Moloch, a cutthroat capitalism, a ruthless ponzi scheme of mega-transnational corporations and their vassals, an engine of mindless cruelty whose sole function is to make the rich richer and the poor poorer, Moloch, ineluctably destined to crush the very concepts of human autonomy and dignity into the black hole of mindless consumption while spewing its waste on the wretched of the earth, debasing and eventually obliterating the very notion of human decency.

How I became confused and how I left my confusion for the clear light of understanding is the subject of my program. My tale. Dissertation. I mean legal brief in support of my claim to competency. The story of my coming to have those thoughts is long and complex, but the story of their departure is short and simple. For it was not a dramatic new medicine, nor a fortuitous encounter with a high-voltage line, nor therapy of any kind that brought me to my senses; it was pure rational introspection. After all, I reasoned, if I were in fact a swarm of honeybees, then I would be neither male nor female. But clearly I am male; I know this by my erections, which I can produce quite easily by looking at the pictures in such magazines as *Erotic X-Films Guide, Leg Show,* and *40+,* for example, or by reading *Penthouse Letters.* Ergo, I am a man, and not a swarm of honeybees. The fact that I am a man and want to fuck anything that jiggles proves that I am not a Shaker village. It is a simple exercise to extend this logic to the case of the vat and the global military-industrial-entertainment complex.

Unless you are as little children you shall not enter the kingdom of heaven, Jesus said, and he was right. So why do we try? We have no more chance of entering heaven than we have of fitting into the clothes we wore to sit on Grandmother's lap. Yet we do try, like so many giants earnestly trying on dolls' dresses and sailor suits, hoping for a miraculous fit. We seek our heaven in this material world or in the spiritual next—most of us, according to a recent survey in *Freemerica Today,* in both.

In our hearts we know that childhood once gone is gone forever, and with it our chance for salvation. Jesus told us in plain Amharic that no grownup's coin hath currency in God's economy. So why do we persist? It is as if we cannot see the pattern that stares us right in the face, as chess-playing computers are unaware of pattern, but achieve their superiority in playing what was once thought to be the most human of games through brute-force enumeration and rank-ordering of sequences of moves, evaluating the best strategy among the billions possible in the time it takes you to mouth the words "I believe." Although chess is an ancient game, it is unlikely that Jesus played it.

It is more likely that he played tag, as children play tag in Bethlehem to this very day. Perhaps, when he was a child, Jesus played tag with Judas. Jesus warned against the dangers of technology and was turned over to the authorities. I'm a stupid man, so I leave theology to the experts. Which brings us back where we started: Bees, Chess, The Nature of Human Consciousness, and a Sad Story of One Brother Who Gave Up Another to the Authorities. What I mean is, I am competent to stand trial. I wish to act as my own attorney.

Because you watch National Public Telescreen you know the story of Alan Turing, the self-terminating British mathematician, code-breaker and lover of boys, from whose fevered brain arose many of the concepts that would later, modulo John Von Neumann, give rise to the digital computer. I am thinking now of the Turing Test, the method he proposed for determining whether a computing device possessed intelligence. Do this, Turing said, in memory of me: put the computer in one room and the (human) tester in another. Have the human interrogate the computer by means of written questions. If, upon reading the answers, the tester cannot tell whether they were written by computer or by fellow human, then the computer can be said to possess intelligence. This is the so-called Turing Test.

People who feel threatened by technology, you among them, Your Honor, viewed the Kasparov/Deep Blue chess contest as a watershed event, a Turing Test that would tell us whether our intelligence had been bested by a machine's. It was no such thing, of course, for chess has never been a measure of humanness. *Story-telling,* not chess, is what makes us human. And we must cling to our humanity no matter what. I am willing to die on the cross to make that point. The day you read a decent novel written by a computer, let me know. Forgive me if I don't hold my breath. I've read them all, more's the pity, and I can tell you that there is not now and never will be a machine that can tell a moving human *short story,* much less a novel.

Now, when I say "novel" I don't mean some thriller about a hard-drinking anti-hero dragged Hitchcock-style into a conspiracy of Silicon Valley computer-biotechnology conglomerates. There are laboratories in picturesque European cities, and awkward doses of the kind of preoccupations you expect from graduate students in electrical engineering and cognitive science: Internet blather and television and sex. *Actions of the Apostate*; bah. That's not what I call a novel.

I mean, rather, Cervantes. Characters palpably human. Stories, that while perhaps farfetched, smack you in the face with their immediacy and truth. Stories that tell you what to do with the longing, desire, regret, in your heart as you fly to Hong Kong, I just picked this up at the airport? Sentences that resonate with the poetry of our days and ways, or it malingers, and not simply rehash garbled syntax some poem you read in high school.

Before I wrote a novel I'd ask what I was walling in or walling out. And before I boasted about a computer-written novel in *this* year, in *this* world, I'd be damn sure it wasn't some novely-novelty-piece, a dog walking on two legs. I'd make damn sure, Betsy, I mean Your Honor, that my so-called novel was accessible but off-balance, crisp, funny, sly but not smug, and always, always, *always* human. Human. Human.

I would strip that motherfucker naked.

In 1983 I lived in Eastboro, New Kent, across the street from the state mental hospital. The male honeybee, by the way, has no stinger and does no work; its sole function in life is to be ready to impregnate the queen on her nuptial flight. It is called a drone. I worked for a computer company at the time and the project I was working on was a floating point (FP) processor.[1] Although I had never had any training[2] in either mathematics or the design of computers, my superior pattern-detecting skills allowed me to discern how a chip or circuit board worked simply by looking at it, and it was easy for me to get a job as head of the FP hardware design team. I am a humble and a social man, but when my electrolytes are imbalanced I tend to display behavior that is sometimes mistaken for arrogance and misanthropy.

The buildings of Eastboro State Hospital were nicely arranged on a campus of a hundred acres or so which jutted into the surrounding Shaker Woods as colonial Jamestown jutted, penis-like, into the Virginia wilderness. Shaker Woods was state property: a tract of two thousand acres that included woodlands (deciduous and evergreen), gardens, meadows, a swamp, and a large freshwater pond. These Woods were like a little Sherwood Forest amid the rapidly developing "technology corridor" of the New Kent computer boom, which was gobbling up the ancient farms of the region at a prodigious rate. Given the demographic pressure of the surrounding area and the popularity of nature-walking among New Kenters, you might have expected the Woods to be thronged with hikers. They were not. For although the land was open to the public it was virtually never used by anyone other than those who called the hospital home: like the fabled forest of Robin Hood's day, the Shaker Woods were superstitiously avoided by the people of the surrounding towns. It was not clear whether this was because they feared the contagion of madness

---

[1] 'Floating point' is a term used to describe a way of representing numbers within a computer's memory. The position of the decimal point 'floats' depending on the number's order of magnitude.

[2] Any training that I could recall, that is. See below.

or if there was some darker reason for their keeping away from the woods. For madness is not catching, after all.

The hospital buildings, which numbered about thirty, were all handsome (if somewhat decrepit); most of them had stood empty for some time. 'Deinstitutionalization' (ghastly word) had seen to that. In addition to the residences, there was an infirmary, a power-generating station, a wood shop, a garage, a barn, and a handful of other buildings whose function was not readily apparent. At the top of the hill stood the Main Hall: a massive vine-covered building of dark red brick. In those days I had a lot more time on my hands, and I used to go for long walks on the hospital grounds, sometimes with my daughter on my back. That's a nice flower; I'll come back for it.

Curiously enough, the State Hospital complex mirrored, in a quasi-fractal fun-house mirror kind of way, the Shaker village of Simplicity, the buildings of which were in fact located on its own forty-acre campus, now virtually overgrown, deep inside the Woods.

{define-class ShakerWoods {inherits Woods}}

Any female larva may become queen.

It was a lovely walk of about half a mile from my house up the hill to the main hall. On the right side of the street, underneath spreading sugar maples neatly spaced, there were six or eight white clapboard houses, each with a porch. On the left side of the street was a gently sloping lawn, and at its far end was a greenhouse. Well they called it a greenhouse but actually it was made out of glass, so technically it was colorless. Beyond the greenhouse lay the pond.

Although the houses were empty, and as I have said, a little in need of paint, still the lawns were mowed, and the greenhouse was in use, so the casual observer—who might have taken a wrong turn on a Sunday drive and gone up the hill in search of a turn-about—might never realized that he was in a forlorn Potemkin village, where New Kent had once, depending on your point of view, either cared for or warehoused its less fortunate.

Some of my friends wondered that I would walk there among the mental patients, especially with a child on my back. But there was nothing to be afraid of: these people were not dangerous, just a little confused sometimes. Sometimes, not all the time. Sometimes. And besides, you hardly ever saw them. Is it a crime to be confused?

The patients (let's not mince words, they were mental patients, not 'clients.' I hate euphemism.); the patients must have lived up at the castle-like Main Hall, but I seldom went by there, so I don't know. Halfway up the hill, right after the field with the greenhouse, there was a little road that branched off and led around the lake: that was the route I usually took on my constitutional promenades. Eventually the road stopped. Beyond the end of the road there was just a little footpath. I could tell you the names of the wild flowers I saw along the way. There were many and they were beautiful. There was no fucking clover.

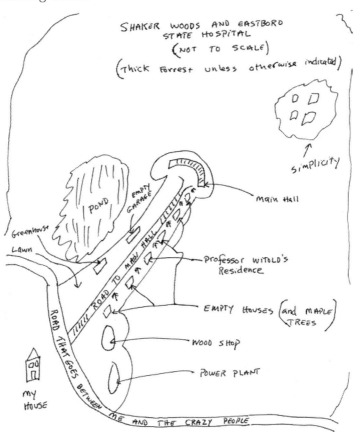

One day in the autumn of 1983 I was walking down that footpath by myself. I was a pipe smoker then; I probably was smoking a pipe.[3] Anyway I was walking down a path, lost in thought when I heard a voice coming from ahead of me. I stopped to listen. By looking ahead though the leaves that obscured a bend in the path, I could make out the form of a woman approaching me. She walked around

---

[3] Smoke has the tendency to make bees lethargic, stupefied. As a man might become after many hours of non-stop masturbation.

the bend looking down and talking to herself. She hadn't seen me and I didn't want to frighten her, so I called out "good day!" She looked up and muttered hello, still walking, then looked down and resumed talking to herself.

I stood to the side to let her pass, and she nearly bumped into me as she walked by. I couldn't make out a word she was saying—she was just kind of droning on, like an old priest saying a Latin Mass in an empty church—a smallish baroque church, with candle-stands holding rose-glassed flickering candles, and dust-covered statues of obscure saints looking down from the half-dome above the altar, Aloysius and Timothy, nestled in alcoves high above the altar—a church to which nobody comes anymore, the people having lost their faith in God, believing 'technology' will save them. The fucking morons. She had gone about ten yards past me—I was watching her—I love to watch women walking away from me—when she stopped and turned and spoke to me.

"Excuse me," she said.

"Yes?"

"This is 1983, right?"

"Yes," I said.

"I was wondering. How would you like for Jesus Christ to come back in 1984?"

She hesitated for a minute, as if somebody were speaking to her, and did one of those Ted Koppel check-the-earpiece motions.

"Along with several other lords," she added.

I took a moment before answering. Remember, this was 1983. How would I like for Jesus Christ to come back in 1984, along with several other lords? Finally I said, "I don't know, but I think I would like it. I think I'd like it a lot."

"Well," she said, "I'm working on it."

Then she walked deeper into the woods. Towards the old barn. Where the goddamned swallows live. And the bats. I hate bats.

So that was 1983 and now it's 1998.

And I am on trial for a crime I did not commit.

Recently I have begun to think a lot about that curious conversation with the woman (presumably a patient of Eastboro State Hospital, although I cannot be certain) in the woods. I remember thinking, as I completed my walk that day, what if she were to be successful in her attempt to bring back Jesus?

And I wonder still. And several other lords, Betsy. What if, indeed, by some process we cannot fathom, what if that crazy woman in the woods were able to bring Jesus Christ Himself back to Earth 'along with several other lords?'

Or to phrase my conjecture another way so as not to offend Christian ears by the implication that Jesus can be summoned anywhere, by anybody, which, presumably, he cannot: what if, on the cusp of the new millennium, what if, whether in response to that woman's prayers or for divine reasons unknowable to us, Jesus, unbeknownst to us, suddenly appeared again on Earth sometime in 1984? After all, that was fourteen years ago. What if?

What if?

An interesting question: for if indeed Jesus Christ did come back to Earth in 1984, where is he now? If he came back the same way he came the first time, that is to say, born of a woman, that would make him about fifteen years old now, skateboarder age, or about as old as Jesus was when he began to astonish his elders in the temple (Luke 4:5-9).

If Jesus is back among us, then, perhaps we should expect to see, any day now, some skateboarder raising holy hell with all the church-going hypocrites who have hijacked his good name.

But who knows?

If Jesus were indeed to come back, would he necessarily come back as a boy? Maybe, like RuPaul, He would choose to be a girl this time.

After all, why can't a girl be a lima bean?

I mean a llama. I mean Lama. I mean a reincarnation of the Deity?

Indeed, if Jesus is divine and can take any form he or she chooses, why would he necessarily come back as a human person at all? What's to say he didn't come back as a dog, or a tiger, or a bee? A honeybee. A thoughtful, loving honeybee, with a stinger loaded with venom ready for that final sacrifice. A bee with personality, a worker, flitting about from flower to flower collecting pollen, not changing water into wine for the marriage feast at Cana but changing pollen into television, I mean honey, telling high-pitched parables to his fellow bees, spreading lovely flower DNA (Dioxyribonucleic Acid, our God and Mother) thinking herky-jerky little Jesus thoughts. A wild-flower honeybee, certainly. Not some boring clover-sniffer all-day-in-the-same-field-with-the-same-job day-in, day-out, the same job, same as anybody else could do, exactly the same, slave-to-the-hive, Bellevue-Washington Digital MicroSystems, no-imagination clover-eating drone.

No.

If Jesus has come back as a honeybee, you will find him among the workers in the wildflowers, not the drones in the clover.

Perhaps he is out there.

Even now.

Upon leaving the woods, I walked home to find that my wife was just finishing up dinner preparations, wearing nothing but black high heels, black stockings, a garter belt, and a lovely black lacy brassiere that could scarcely contain her softball-sized breasts. I quickly put my son to bed and got down to the hard business of undoing transglobal capitalism, thwarting the nefarious plans of the High Druid of Informationtology, and derailing a crackpot cybermilitia. `Reset`. I mean I got down to some activities, which are documented in my article "Vegetable Hijinks" in *Lusty Letters,* volume 1 no. 4.

As I recall, it was only a short while after my encounter with the Jesusmancer in the woods—a few months, perhaps—that Dr. Thadeus Witold took up residence in the third of the hitherto abandoned residences on the road towards the main hall of Eastboro State Hospital.

Dr. Witold, a credentialed psychiatrist of great renown, had just arrived from the famous Polish city of Gdansk (otherwise known as Danzig, which is the source of the family name of Georg Danzig, he of simplex algorithm fame, the 'linear programming' algorithm behind the stunning logistical miracle of the supply of the allied armies in World War II, which, as much as any noble sacrifice on the shores of Omaha Beach or Iwo Jima, lay behind the defeat of the Nazi Moloch).[4]

Dr. Witold had been specifically recruited by the Medical Director of Eastboro State Hospital to deal with the extremely recalcitrant case of the so-called King of Zembla, who was reputedly confined in restraints in the attic of the Main Hall. This royal fellow,

---

[4]Danzig's simplex algorithm, by the way, is a beautiful thing but it is very sensitive to floating point errors. A result that was off by as little as a single digit in the ninth decimal place could cause the Army supply corps to send bullets to the kitchen and boatloads of Idaho potatoes to men lying on the beach under fire, calling 'ammo!'

though insane, was evidently a genius of some sort. Through proxies this 'King of Zembla' had negotiated for special treatment in return for which he promised to divulge some vital information relating to Freemerican national security. Accordingly he had been moved, strait-jacketed, to his top-floor suite, from which he could look down on the entire Shaker Woods as if it were his private demesne.

I met Dr.Witold on one of my long walks, as I have said, with my daughter, sometime that winter (1983-1984) which was curiously lacking in snow. He was unpacking his belongings from a car—a rather beat-up grey Pinto covered with bumper stickers that said things like *"Afghanistan=Russian Graveyard,"* which I thought was rather shameful: the hospital or the rental agency should have procured a car more befitting a man of his stature, but let that go—and, kind neighbor that I am, I stopped to give him a hand, lugging his fucking bullshit, I covered her tits with about a gallon of jism into the house. **Reset.**

I guess maybe because I was thinking about the Shakers. Some people have the mistaken impression that their founder, Ann Lee, was taken by her followers to be some kind of second coming of Jesus. This is something neither she nor the Shakers ever said or believed. So if you're keeping a scorecard of American Religious Sects that Believe they have Witnessed the Reincarnation, you can scratch the Shakers off your list. They did not believe that Mother, as they called her, was Jesus. They believed, rather, that she had brought the *spirit of Christian love* to Earth once again. In this belief they were profoundly correct. I know the name of that flower, I just cannot think of it at the moment. Why was I thinking about the Shakers? Who knows. Why does one think the things one thinks? Listen to Marvin Kinsky and all these artificial intelligence so-called 'experts' and they'll start talking about 'memes' that replicate just as 'genes' do, and they'll talk *computational aspects of cognition,* and *directly introspected epistemic correlates of neurologic state changes.* Fancy talk for fancy people. Certainly the Shakers were not fancy people. They were bee keepers. And celibate. Provably so. No sex. Virgins.

Shakers had a lot in common with bees. The sense of community. The celibacy. The elegant solutions; simplicity. The willingness of the individual to sublimate his or her identity into the whole. Also both of these community forms are diurnal. I'm getting a little bit hungry.

When I was overseas all those many years ago, trying to help the village to better organize itself, I had no notion of Shakers. Now

I wish that I had. You see, it's the cleanliness thing, the sweeping out of the hive; the meeting room, the Shaking dance. It's the way civilized people take care of each other. I'm really rather hungry.

What I'm trying to say is that the Shakers were kind of a prototype and early embodiment of an efficient capitalist system of Internet-connected global free trade hives, I mean partners, unimpeded by sentimental protectionism and namby-pamby human-rights rhetoric. Her tits with about a gallon of jism, and she loved every drop.

Gatorade™.

Namby-pamby human rights. Her tits with about a gallon of. Internet. Gatorade™.

When my electrolytes get out of whack I can get confused. I can usually detect this with my diagnostics and reset myself. That's because of the quality of my built-in sytems test. But if the state persists for too long the BIST's parser seizes up. If the parser seizes up I have to go through the whole process of flushing all the buffers and resetting, which takes forever, and during this resetting I am in kind of an indeterminate state, like a waking sleep. The best thing to do is, if you see me acting a little confused, open the lid and pour in about a gallon of Gatorade.

In 1984 I was still working at MiniComputer Inc., in Eastboro. I was a technical writer, which means that I took specs—specifications—that read something like this:

```
CK10 This arms strobe; if nul de-
faults to the value in STROBVAL rom.
CK11. Not used. CK12 if 1 increments
slave clock by 3 milliseconds.
```

And turned them into something that read like this:

Partake as doth the bee

Abstemiously

A rose is an estate

In Sicily

That was a joke. I turned specs into prose, not poetry. I leave poetry for the virgins of Amherst, Massachusetts. And I'm no virgin. Not me, brother. But oh boy, I could tell you some stories. Virgins? Christ.

Anyway in 1984 I was working at MiniComputer Inc., that same place that Stacy Kidd wrote about in his Pulitzer Prize-winning book *The Soul of a New Computer*. What's that one called, with the blue petals? You see it by roadsides a lot; I think it must like gravel or road salt. Well, pardon me, Stacy, but a computer is a machine, and machines do not have souls.

Yes, I know, I know; you were speaking metaphorically, the *soul of the machine* was the *people who invented it*, who worked long hours in the basement of MiniComputer Inc., to bring the machine to life, so to speak. Who worked long hours, sometimes not seeing their wives or children (their beautiful children whose hearts are pure and trusting, whether in their clean safe beds in New Kent, or lying in the mud in the hell-hole of the Earth), working like bees the live-long day, reading specs, writing specs, writing code—system code I'm talking about here, none of your BASIC crap—and trying to figure out that fucking floating point bug, that goddamn floating point bug that went away if you heated the board with a hair dryer or cooled it with a hit of Freon. Who the hell could have figured out that beast of a bug? It went away with heat or cold! It was a crazy goddamn bug, and it could have happened to anybody. That's no reason to assign a chip designer to write a software manual, for God's sake.

So that's what you meant by *Soul of a New Computer*: the people. OK, I get it, already. But let me tell you something, Stacy Pulitzer Prize Kidd. You led a lot of people astray. And now, thanks to you, a lot of people really believe that machines do have souls, and they sit in the center of their little hives in Bellevue, Washington and the rest of us feed them honey. So that's what I think about machines and souls.

I forgot to say, when you put in the Gatorade™, make sure you read the label, because the solder flux bottle looks somewhat similar, and if you throw that in, the whole tank turns into a giant radio receiver and there's no way I can shut it off.

Anyway Tom Best, the putative hero of your Pulitzer Prize-winner, was a handsome charismatic guy, I'll give you that much. I stood in awe of him, like he was John Lennon or something. One day he came to the staff meeting of the Technical Writing group and he gave a little talk. At that point in time, you remember (1983), the microprocessor hadn't yet won the day and seemingly intelligent people were still building CPUs with bit slice technology. It's true. You can't make this stuff up.

Well, in the days just before Tom's visit to our group, a couple more guys had just left our engineering team to go join Zeus Computer Inc., up in Chelmsford. They were going to build workstations, which was the hot new idea at the time. But they weren't going to design their own CPU. They were going to buy 68000's from Motorola and build the rest of their logic around that. What's that one called, with the black in the middle, and yellow petals? People put them in their gardens, but I think they're ugly. Taste like crap, too.

So Tom Best comes in to give us a little pep talk, boost our morale, tell us where the company's going, what the product strategy is, all that good stuff. The Corporation wanted to keep us computer engineers motivated, you understand, so we wouldn't defect to this new start-up Zeus Computer, Inc. Obviously: MiniComputer Inc. couldn't survive if all its best engineers got up and left for Zeus, now could it? And a technical writer is, of course, an engineer.

So there we are in the conference room, all of us technical writers, all of us Award of Distinguished Technical Communication winners, and Tom goes to the white board and he draws a line that slopes from lower left to upper right, and at each endpoint he writes one of the code names for two machines that were under development at the time. Hawk and Heron. Heron and Hawk. Neither of these birds is a bee eater.

And he says, "Let me explain product strategy. You got your low end; that's the Heron," he points to the low end of the line. "And you got your high end; that's the Hawk." He points to the high end. "And then you got all this baroque shit in the middle." He waves his hand vaguely at the board.

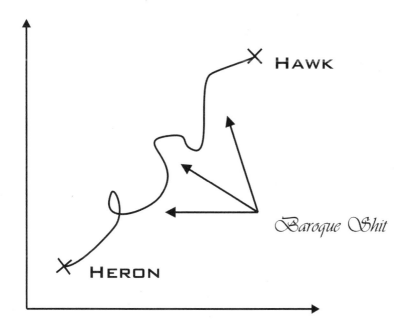

Product Strategy

Then he says, "OK, that's enough about product strategy. Let's talk about Zeus. You've all heard about Zeus, this new start-up. Or if you haven't heard about it you should get out of here, because you're probably fucking useless. So, Zeus. What's their story? They're going to put a sixty-eight thousand on a board and sell it as a computer. That's their product strategy. Let me repeat that. They're going to buy a chip ready-made in a box full of sawdust, they're going to stick it on some printed circuit board, and they're going to call that their computer."

He hesitates for a few seconds, like he's looking for the right words to convey the full measure of his disdain.

"Now, if somebody wants to take a chip and stick it on a board..." he says, and this look of disgust comes over his face, "and they want to call themselves a *computer designer,* well I guess that's their business." Then he looks up, and the sour look goes off his face—now he's brightening, and pretty soon he looks like George C. Scott in *Patton,* ready to rally us. "But that's not what we call computer engineering at MiniComputer Inc.!" he yells, "And if I can find some way to cut them off at the knees, I'm going to do it!"

So you can see how he was a funny guy, and an inspiring one as well. I mean he still is. I guess. I don't know. I saw him at a trade show in San Francisco a few years ago; he was wearing a blue blazer that showed just a hint of dandruff. It was like, Uniforum, or some loser trade show like that. It was at a time when we nerds still ruled the net, Betsy, before the suits won. Tom was still handsome but a little paunchy. I was dropping hints for a job, but he wasn't catching them. Where am I going? I hate these big trucks, the wind-wash blows you half a mile into some damn alfalfa or something. What is this, clover? I've never seen it up close. I don't usually come by here. I mean I don't *ever* come by here. I've never been here in my life. But if some damn truck blows you right on top of the flower, for Christ's sake...

Anyway, I hardly knew Tom Best in 1984, and I was in awe of him, like he was John Lennon or something. Herky-Jerky. And well, I needed to make more money. I had children; I had a brain that was in serious risk of atrophy. I had a soul. Stacy, are you listening? I had a soul? I was a person, not a machine, and I had a soul. Aaand so anyway at the time MiniComputer Inc. had just purchased this entire campus from a defunct Catholic woman's college, in Woodstock, Rhode Island, and they were setting it up as a training facility. A training facility, I say. A god-damned training facility. Where we could go learn more engineering, good God, as if we didn't know how to design computers already. I don't want to hear about that floating point bug. One floating point bug doesn't mean that one does not know how route a circuit board.

I was going to debug Kali, or die trying.

Thirty-six strobe lines—an electroencephalogram of the Kali chip's brain waves—danced in parallel from left to right across the four monochrome monitors in my cluttered office. The answer to the riddle lay hidden within them, and I knew that if I looked hard enough I would eventually find it. Unless, of course, I went mad first.

So the whole engineering group (including one lowly technical writer who it just so happens could have designed the socks off of half the so-called engineers in the division) piled into a couple of buses and headed down to Woodstock for a couple of days of training.

I'm waiting for you to laugh.

Don't you get it?

Am I the only one who finds this ironic? A bunch of *nerds* going to *Woodstock* on a *bus*? Where a religious school has gone bust and has been taken over by the soul of a machine? Technology our new God and Woodstock our seminary? Oh nevermind. Clover. It doesn't taste that bad. But bland, bland, bland. If I had to live on a steady diet of this stuff I would sting myself and die.

So the first day at Woodstock was all presentations by engineering project leads. "Our team is using programmable array logic for the I/O." "We're looking into associative memory..." Blah blah blah. There were only five women in our engineering group. Three of them were plain janes, but two of them were knock-outs. I mean, what I wouldn't have given to... So that's where my mind was: women. Sort of. Really my mind was somewhere else: I was thinking about my plan. I had a project that I wanted to propose to Tom Best, but I was very nervous about it. This was long before anybody else was talking about doing an actual Consciousness-Transfer. Now that it's commonplace people tend to forget how revolutionary it was at the time.

So of course I was very horny. I mean nervous. I was very nervous, and I needed to sell my idea to Tom. How far is it from here to Bellevue, do you think? There was to be a dinner that night in the school, I mean training facility, cafeteria, and afterwards there was to be a party with a live "rock 'n roll" band. I put 'rock 'n roll' in quotes because it was a nerdo band, drones with electric guitars trying to pretend that they weren't nerds: "This isn't the real me," they were trying to say, in their own stylized drono-nerdo way, "the nerd you see before you isn't the real me. The real me is a rock star." Give me a break. They were clover-drinkers, every one of them. Where do you want to go today?

Where do I want to go today? I want to go to Montana.

There was liquor at this party, see, well, beer anyway, which is what I prefer, being a guy, and I drank one bottle of it to fortify my nerves. I'm not afraid to admit that I was nervous about approaching Tom. It really was a revolutionary idea that I was going to sell him on, and I was afraid that he might reject it before he really understood it. Also, as I have said, I am fundamentally stupid, a stupid little box, which means that while I can see the patterns, the deep deep patterns of existence, I cannot explain to people even such simple things as why one plus one equals two (which makes it odd that I am a writer). People with no vision would have said I was crazy, and I was afraid that Tom might come to the same conclusion. Not another truck! Jesus Christ, slow down, wouldya? Now here I am back here again! Clover. Give me a break.

So I drank a beer, just one, and then I was on my way over to introduce myself to him. I was just going to introduce myself to him, I was this close, but of course Shareena got there just ahead of me and started talking to him, and Betsy, and why in the hell an engineer, a so-called engineer, would pack a dress like that to wear to a three-day engineering retreat is beyond me; you don't pack something like that unless you want men looking down between your breasts, imagining their heads nestled there, between them, their left hand now cups your right breast and twists it ever-so-gently—it's firm, like an avocado, but with care it can be twisted, just enough for that man's tongue to reach out and find the nipple, those little bumps around the push-pin, his right hand slides up the back of her right leg, she opens, he puts a finger in, she is wet, wet like a field of clover, I mean like a field of wild flowers after a spring rain.

So I had another beer. Well, a few more beers. I looked over to Tom, and you guessed it: there was Betsy, there was Shareena, still yakking about bit-slice technology. I caught Tom's eye; it was obvious that he was anxious to talk with me but was unable to pry himself free of those two beautiful busty long-legged wet-lipped logic designers. I was getting more and more nervous. I had to see Tom, and I couldn't wait all night. I had to explain my idea to him, to make him see the potential. We would invent a whole new technology, Tom and I. He had to get me out of technical writing and put me back on a hardware design team. He had to give me a team of my own, in fact. I needed to make more money. I needed to fix up my house. It was starting to look like one of the abandoned residences at Eastboro State where the clients used to reside. I mean patients. I mean, the, what's the word. Nut-cases. Mostly, however, I needed to save the human race from its own folly, by the expedient of a simple piece of technology.

But getting back to Tom and the women. When would he ever get free of them? He glanced at me again, where I was standing patiently over by the bar, avoiding all the boring nerdo chit-chat. All of a sudden I thought, oh God, *maybe he doesn't want to get free of them.* Maybe he was imaging his tongue, too, on Betsy's nipple; maybe he was thinking of *two* sets of breasts, *four* push-pin nipples, and those sweeter-tasting push-pins, those erasers down below in the clover field. You know what I mean. The wild flower field. Could Tom have been interested in sex? I didn't think so.

How can anybody live on clover alone? I don't know. It tends to make one feel heavy, too.

Like I said, this all took place in 1984.

From an early age I had dreaded the arrival of that year. Because of the Orwell novel, of course, the novel *1984*, which my cousin Christian Friedrich Bremser forced me to read when I was ten years old. So ever since reading that book I had feared the Queen Bee. I mean Big Brother. That all-pervasive, all knowing, intrusive, lying, truth-twisting, spying, mind-fucking, self-serving, life-sapping, bee-enslaving, amorphous technology-crazed autonomy-hating freedom-quashing materialistic thing. Moloch. I feared it, loathed it. If you'll pardon the illusion, allusion, as Ahab feared and loathed the Whiteness of the Whale. So even then, in 1984, although I was a grown man, and not a virgin, far from it, a grown man—with children, remember?—I still had a vestigial fear about that year. I was afraid that something was going to go terribly wrong, like swallows at mid-day. But 1984 came and went, and 1985 and 1986 too, and nothing happened. Even up until now, nothing has happened. Orwell was wrong. So we're safe.

I can't remember the name of this pink flower on this vine. It's pretty though, isn't it? I am very sensitive to beauty. Especially the beauty of women. And of wildflowers, like this one. I'll come back for it when I'm not so full. That is why women, in general, find me so attractive—because of my sensitivity. Especially when it comes to sex. I am the kind of lover women dream of, because I seek neither my own satisfaction nor yet theirs, but ours, a new thing, marvelous and instantaneous, intensely real but soon gone, and the more precious for its evanescence. (Not that I think of women in that way any more, I hasten to add, being married. I'm talking about how I used to regard women when I was single. Today I'm a married man, so if I happen to cast my eye upon some beautiful woman, say, as we chance to meet in the playground of the East Kent school at two-forty-five as we each wait for our children to be excused, Hi June! Hi Kate! I never experience lustful thoughts about her. But before I was married? Well, let's just say I could tell you some stories and leave it at that.) Now here comes old Fivelegs, telling me to fly home. Screw you. I'll go home when I feel like it. I'm my own drone. OK you lead I'll follow.

At last I saw Tom Best go outside, and I followed after him, to try to find a minute to talk to him, casual-like. And there he was in the moonlight, and the streetlight glinting off his glasses made him look a little like John Lennon, and I was in awe of him, but there must have been some poison in the dinner, or something, because even though that breeze at first felt good, within a few moments I was, well, let's not use euphemisms, I hate euphemism, I was vomiting, rather, I was puking my fucking guts out into the bushes. I went back to the dorm to recoup, where, after rinsing my mouth with clover juice, I mean flower nectar, I mean mouthwash, I went to bed.

In the morning I woke up and changed my underwear.

The next day it was more of the same, Soul of a New Computer-wise. More computer talk, more women to look at. Who was it that was wearing that short-short dress? I don't remember who, right now, whose long legs they were, with oh! what calves, good God in heaven what calves, crossed there, just so, just so, that right ankle hooked around the left, no; left around the right...

If you insist on crossing this road at this altitude, Fivelegs, you will meet the same fate as Squishy, the windshield boy. OK you lead I'll follow.

So I stayed in my seat like a good little drone. I did not go over to her and say, 'please, please may I run my tongue up your leg, until you tell me just where and how to taste and drink?' No. I watched and listened to the presentation about all the baroque shit in the middle, and at lunch I went back to my dorm room and changed my underwear.

Jeez, what a backwash. What did I tell you. Are you OK, Fivelegs? Fivelegs? Hey, where are you? Oh, good Christ. Now how am I going to get home?

After lunch there were more meetings, punctuated by a volleyball game at three, and the reason I was staring at Betsy's breasts, in this instance, was emphatically not prurient: they were large, and I was concerned that she might sprain them, inasmuch as she appeared to be wearing only her regular bra, and not the sports variety that holds them, like a hand, a loving hand, and it was in that spirit that I made my offer, I would like to again state that for the record, Your Honor.

That afternoon, after the game, the agenda called for a lecture on "Product Engineering Process," but Tom tricked us: instead giving us the boring lecture that we expected he showed us a movie, called *Gizmo*, that featured old black and white newsreel clips of crazy inventors of foolish inventions. And how we laughed at that movie! We laughed until the tears ran down our faces, me and the computer-engineering nerds as well, at one foolish never-could-work invention after another in the old black and white clips: baby-rockers, diaper changers, tea-kettle pourers, clothes-put-er-on-ers, and on, and on: hopeless attempts to fly, enormous contraptions that collapsed under their own weight, bird-shaped aeroplanes that fell like bricks from their launching pads, people dressed as birds jumping out of trees, a panoply of hope besting reason leading to failure again and again and again.

And then: color.

A snowy mountaintop, a man strapped into a hang glider, wearing skis. Down he schusses, ever faster. Down, accelerating, the only sound his skis on snow (growing fainter as he recedes and friction ceases) until the wind catches and lifts him, and he flies free in the air like any bird, or bee. High into the sky he flies, as high as the virgin queen on her nuptial flight, swirling ever higher, athletically maneuvering like the drone who has waited for her since birth, growing ever hornier with the drone's own God-given need to fuck, comprehending it not, the only male of his swarm who will ever know the ecstasy of mating—and pay for the knowledge instantaneously with his life—and he floats, and soars. And the gooseflesh was on my arms, and the tears of awe and happiness flowed from my eyes—not only for this one man's triumph, nor even for mankind's: it was my own triumph that gave me such joy. For clearly this film was Tom's way of speaking to me, of telling me that though others might think my ideas were crazy and laugh at me, yet Tom knew that I was the one, who, having studied and learned from the naive attempts of my predecessors, would soar. I would be the one, the first human to ever successfully transfer consciousness from a carbon form to a silicon form. I resolved that I would talk with him that night and let nothing deter me.

Alas that night unfolded as had the one before: the same women monopolizing Tom's every moment. The same smiles—in demure, red wet lipstick; the same curves of the necks turned away from me, the same shoulders, arms and narrow wrists, the same inviting mountainsides sloping from shoulders down to hidden breasts; the same waists, a braceletted hand resting on one; the same rounded behinds in tight dresses; thighs, calves, ankles, toes and soles of feet. Again I drank, waiting my main chance. Again upon my stepping outside the night air interacted with the food from the contaminated kitchen; again the sickness overcame me as Tom stood there, like John Lennon. He must not have noticed me falling.

I awoke in the morning, in a pool of my own sickness, in a field of flowers.

Lying there, in stillness, I saw a gorgeous butterfly alight on a stamen of a bright red flower, whose name is... well, nevermind. I reached out my hand in the childlike hope that the butterfly might come to me. But just as it was about to leave for its new perch on my finger, however, an obnoxious bee, out of nowhere, alighted on my nose and stung me, which made me recoil in pain (while paradoxically at the same instant I felt a momentary but pleasurable swelling of my penis), and the butterfly flew away.

By the time I found my way back to the dormitory room the buses had left and my suitcase (including all my underwear but minus my magazines), was sitting on the curb. It took me two days to hitchhike from Rhode Island back to New Kent, and when I got there I found out that there had been a layoff, and that despite all of Tom Best's entreaties, the mindless corporate bureaucrats had insisted that my name remain on the list of sacrificial victims to the implacable god of Shareholder Value, and my days at MiniComputer Inc. were over.

Oh, there's that yellow flowery bush, whatchamacallit. I think I can find my way from here.

Imagine, for a moment, that you are an inventor, and you have set for yourself the task of inventing a story-telling machine. You build something; you turn it on. It speaks, in words unmistakably English, using syntax largely correct. Have you done what you set out to do? Is this sequence of words a story? How will you decide whether or not you have succeeded? Here is a proposal.

A story-telling machine, to be worthy of the name, must be able to at least pass the Trurl/Kalapachus test, which simply states that any machine that is to be called a story-telling machine must produce at least one story that at least one listener (or reader, if the story is in written form) can follow from start to finish, with the further provisos that the story be at least as long as *Goodnight Moon* and not be about a lonely housewife from the Midwest who gives meaning to her life through an impetuous affair.

The problems in building such a device would lie not so much in the NLP, the natural language processor, as in the associative memory. Telling a time sequence without veering off on a million tangents thereby losing the narrative thread and controlling voice. Telling me with a knowing look that she had noticed the bulge in my trousers, which could scarcely conceal my ten inch man-muscle ready to speak to her love-exerciser in a language it wouldn't soon forget. **Reset.** To tell a story is to convey a pattern of meaning. Pattern recognition is a particularly human skill. Machines are not so good at it. Because they have no soul. I do not know the meaning of my life. Fucking moron. `Reset`.

The meaning of the life of the bee is, however, quite clear. The meaning of the life of the bee is hope: hope made visible, audible, tangible. That is the meaning of the life of the bee. To explain how this is so is beyond my poor powers; however, you have only to go to your library and obtain a copy of *The Life of the Bee*, by Maeterlink, and read it, for he explains it all, moreover, in a voice so direct, personable, earnest, and intelligent—as rendered in the elegant translation of Sutro—that you will feel, in reading it, as a bee must feel in eating honey, which, Maeterlink tells us, to the bee is "liquid life," so perfectly adapted to the bee's needs that there is virtually no waste from it.

I know too the meaning of the Shaker village. The meaning of the Shaker village is Heaven:

> *My heavenly home is here*
> *No longer need I wait*
> *To cross the foaming river*
> *Or pass the pearly gate*
> *I've angels all around me*
> *With kindness they surround me*
> *To a glorious cause they've bound me*
> *And my heavenly home is here*

For Shakers did not believe in life beyond the grave. They believed in Heaven on Earth, which can be defined as having their electrolytes never out of balance, which is to say as being in a state of perpetual love, and they believed that they were living in Heaven. And they *were* living in Heaven. That is the meaning of a Shaker village. The Shakers lived in twenty communities in nine states, and although there is an unmistakable commonality of purpose and sensibility among all twenty, yet still each village had its own personality. My own personality veers from charming to revolting, depending on the electrolytes.

I know the names of many, many flowers. Perhaps as many as a thousand. If I cannot think of the name of this little purple and white doobie, with this stem that looks so limp even when freshly watered, it is only a passing thing. Sometimes I cannot recall even my own mother's name, but I know who she is. That is to say, as an abstract statement I know who my mother is.

After having lost my position at MiniComputer Inc., it was imperative that I get back to work on a floating point board—for reasons that I will soon make clear. Time was running out, not just for me, but for the entire human race.

It was clear that I would have to go to get a job at Zeus Computer Inc. But knowing that my defection would be a setback to MiniComputer Inc. and a personal blow to Tom Best, who had recently been so magnanimous to me, I thought it only decent to tell Tom of my decision face to face, antennae to antennae. I went down to the GoodBurger at the corner, where they have a telephone.

By chance Betsy was in Tom's office when I called and it was she who answered his phone. She answered breathlessly, as if in anticipation of hearing my voice—and distinctly said "Oh, shit," when she found out that it was indeed I who was on the line. She didn't have to finish her words, which strong emotion had obviously caused to catch in her throat: "Oh shit, Paavo, it's just terrible the way they laid you off." Clearly she still had feelings for me, and had long since forgotten our little misunderstanding about the sports bra at the volleyball game. I find that a little bit of honey, after a long exertion, whether mental or physical, greatly refreshes. After a judicious serving of honey, neither too large or too small, one's thoughts are clearer, one's reasoning facilities are more trustworthy, and one's sentences have a more graceful cadence. Elder John reports an ample supply for the coming winter, when the bees will be quiet.

Tom's advice was prescient: "There's always turnover in this business, so why don't you take a breather for a little while until an opening comes up? I'll bet it won't be long," he said, then added with a knowing tone, "I'm sure you and that wife of yours can find ways to pass the time."

I took his advice, and in the weeks leading up to that awful automobile accident that took the lives of the entire Zeus floating point team I found plenty to do. For starters, I caught up on my reading. I had whole stacks of *JugTown, Girls Only, Nasty Letters,* and *Adult Film Preview* that I hadn't even browsed, let alone given the kind of attention they merited. I had my wife to take care of (and let me tell you, once she gets going you can forget about doing much else). Then there was my son to play with. I mean my daughter. My child.[5] But the other thing I did with those few weeks of unplanned vacation was to get to know my new neighbor, Dr. Witold.

At first my visits to him were simple neighborliness: it was clear that his experiences behind the Iron Curtain had been traumatic, and he had not quite accustomed himself to his newfound freedom. This was apparent from the way he concealed the shabby rental car behind the house, covering it with bracken; by the way he pretended not to be home when I knocked on his door (still remembering, no doubt, those terrible nighttime visits by the secret police in those years before the Venzig wall came down), by his never using electricity (not realizing that in our country it is free), and so on. Now that he was safe in Freemerica, I thought it was only proper to help him feel more comfortable, and so I went to see him. With time our friendship grew.

What a marvelous therapeutic way he had! He has. Still has. It was easy to see why the Medical Director of Eastboro State Hospital had recruited him to help that poor Zemblan client, I mean nut-case, that deposed monarch in restraints atop the Hill House. Dr. Witold's words were few, but therefore all the more precious. When he spoke each word was as laden with wisdom as a comb is laden with honey.

"Hey," Dr. Witold said to me one day, as I was explaining to him (or should I say trying to explain to him, I am so poor with words) the nature of the floating point bug and the fate of the world, "Hey, what the fuck is your problem?"

It was as if he had unlocked the door which had kept so much inside of me for so long. Such simple words, and yet conveyed with such feeling. I don't know how to properly express what I felt under his masterly spell. I sat down, collected my wits, and told him the story of my life.

---

[5] I have a child. Several children actually. I think I have mentioned him or her, that I love to go places with, play with, teach, help to grow and learn. How I love to hear that child of mine say, "Daddy, let's play."

The story of my life. I fell into confusion and climbed out. The story of my life. Nasty, brutish and short. The story of my life. A drone trapped in a worker's body. The story of my life. A white white man in a black black world. The story of my life. A Shaker village swallowed by a wood. The story of my life. A linear equation in a quadratic world. GOSUB BACKSTORY.

BACKSTORY:
REM: Tom says this is dead code. Will pay $100 if it ever executes.
REM: Uncomment this code when publishing CCD

I was born into a typically Freemerican family, with a typically Freemerican mother and father (whom I called "Mom" and "Dad," respectively) and an average number of brothers and sisters. I had a typical childhood, in one of the Freemerican states.

I was just a child when our beloved martyred beekeeper John Fitzpatrick O'Toole took up the beekeeper's veil, and I can still remember his inaugural speech, those stirring words spoken with that perfect Katharine Hepburn quaver in his voice, "Ask not what your apiary can do for you, ask what you can do for your apiary!" It was only several months later that he issued his call to Freemerican youth to join the "Hey, Why Can't We All Just Get Along? Corps." And as soon as I was old enough to join, I did.

I have no heroic stories to tell of my time overseas. I spent five years in Sahelia trying to do what was right in the name of human decency (and Freemerica), and then I came home.

That is, I tried to come home. I did come back to Freemerica, but home, like deep thought, eluded me. It eludes me still. For years, as a Hey, Why Can't We All Just Get Along? Corps volunteer I thought often of home. I remembered friends, family, places; a girlfriend: the usual. And I spent countless idle hours imagining our joyful reunions. But when I made my return—when, after having spent five years living in the small village of Tanaye along the Tenegal river in the impossibly poor country of Sahelia—after five years of sleeping on a straw mat in a mud hut, of taking my water from a hand-dug well, of working with farmers to improve their seeds and use of fertilizer, of annual visits to the capital city of Tabour, each time more dazzled, more of a bumpkin—after five years of that I came back here.

But the instant that I placed my foot upon Freemerican terra firma I found that I could recall neither my mother's name nor my father's, nor the state of my birth, nor my childhood friends, nor my brothers or sisters, and I found that I could not imagine how these people that I saw all about me, scurrying like bees at a picnic—I could not imagine how I had ever had anything to do with them, nor could I imagine how I ever might again. Yet keenly I could recall my homesickness for them, not just my family and friends, but for all Freemericans; I knew that until the very moment that the plane from Sahelia had touched down at JFO International Airport I had been rehearsing in my mind the stories I would tell, the questions I would ask. But once I was off that airplane, once I faced the actualities of Freemerica herself, my mind went blank.

There I stood, at the baggage claim carousel of JFO International Airport, unable to recall my own given name. For years, following the self-effacing custom of the HWCWAJGAC volunteer, I had gone by my Sahelian name ('Ntrog 'Nkoolan) and I had actually forgotten my Freemerican (English) name; I was worried that I would not be able to figure out which luggage was mine. Then the problem solved itself: there was only one suitcase left, slowly revolving around the carousel in the empty cavernous hall. The name tag said Paavo Nurmi, which sounded somehow familiar, and I soon concluded that it was my own luggage, therefore I knew that I was called Paavo Nurmi. But now all I had was a name. I needed to recall who I was. I sat down on the bag and tried to conjure up my Freemerican self.

I could not do it. The harder I tried to recall the experiences of my youth, the stronger my Sahelian experience fought back, as if it were a giant magnet of like polarity. If, say, I tried to bring to my mind a memory of playing Little League baseball on a beautiful Saturday morning in June, I would recall instead a blind girl dressed in rags, led by her brother to beg in the streets of Tabour. "It's cold," she said with a smile, tasting the Coca Cola I bought for her. *Enna boubi.* If I tried to recall a birthday party, perhaps beside a suburban pool, with barefoot children in party hats, waiting to sing and swim, I would only be able to recall the barefoot children of Tanaye, singing while running down the rats, stomping them to death before they could escape tothe river as the sun set. If I tried to remember seagulls at the beach on a family trip to Florida, I would only see the plague of birds that came in swarms so thick they caused darkness at noon, and I would remember the sound they made (like an Atlas rocket) taking off en masse from a ruined field of sorghum. If I tried to recall whether I had a little brother or sister, I could only remember little Amadou, who died of starvation in my arms.

With nowhere to go and nothing to do, I sat in an uncomfortable airport chair and opened my bag. There were a few sets of clothes, which oddly didn't seem my size, and several books: *Linear Programming*, *The Design of Math Co-Processors*, *Floating Point Specification 801.2*, and several others of that nature. I read them all.

I left the airport, bought a car, took possession of the house on Lyman street, married a gorgeous gal, perfect, really: a great cook, really swell conversationalist, physicist, with tits the size of softballs that tasted like honey, sweet thick honey; and I got a job as a designer of computer hardware. But there was a void in my life: I knew not who I was.

Yet I had only to get in a car and drive towards the airport, as if I were to be heading back to Sahelia, and the memories would start to shift back in, and the closer I got to the actual plane that might be able to lift me back to the poor I had left behind the stronger and more varied the memories of my youth became. And if I went so far as to purchase a ticket for a flight to Tabour, the capital city of Sahelia, the memories of my youth, my friends, my family would overwhelm my senses, as a strong pounding rain overwhelms the concrete-hard soil of a drought-stricken land. Then I would return the ticket for a refund and the memories would begin to dim, as a flood recedes. Yet never would I have the presence of mind, under that flash-flood of memories, to write down any clues that I could use to guide me back to myself once I had left the airport and the memories had again vanished completely. Indeed, so strong and vivid were the memories at the time, like a butterfly's dream that it is a man—it cannot conceive of waking up—that I could not imagine their ever fading again. But once I left the airport grounds and circled back towards the entrance to the New Kent Throughway the memories faded and jostled into each other, and by the time I returned to my house in Eastboro, across the street from the hospital, all I knew of my own history was that I had been born into a typically Freemerican family, with a typically Freemerican mother and father, whom I called "Mom" and "Dad" respectively, and an average number of brothers and sisters. I had a typical childhood, in one of the Freemerican states. And the only true and vivid memory of my youth was the quavering Katherine Hepburn voice *ask not what your apiary can do for you...*

It was a most particular amnesia: I could recall my time in Sahelia quite vividly, more or less from the time of my arrival there until my departure five years later. Like all memory, my Sahelian memory was incomplete and tended to modify itself on re-fresh. (`This is a simple refresh logic problem. Get Pavel to work on it.`) But as far as human memory goes (it's not as if I'm a machine, after all), my memory was pretty good. I could re-call leaving Sahelia and my return to Freemerica: everything about it—from the handful of Lomotil that I ingested before boarding the jet at the Tabour airport to the shock I felt upon seeing so many white people at JFO, the taste of the coffee, the baseball on the television in the airport bar: the wonderful sensation of being home. Such a simple thing as a Freemerican newsstand: after five years of government-con-trolled press in Sahelia—a diet as bland as pure clover—how grand it was to see a Freemerican news vendor: the First Amendment and bee enterprise rolled into one person, standing beside his splendid collec-tion of newspapers and magazines resplendent behind him like a field of wild flowers: *The New Kent Times, The Wall Street Journal, For-eign Affairs, BeesWeek, Sports Illustrated, Sports Illustrated Swimsuit Edition, Playboy, Penthouse, Investors Business Daily, Penthouse Forum, Penthouse Letters, Girls of Penthouse, High Society, Baron's, Stacked, TitCity, HoneyPot, X-o-Ramma, Sexville, Money, Sexfest, Sexmag, Fortune, Sexopia, Couples Humping, Forbes, MensaBabes, Fuckfest...*

I started my new life, working on the floating point proces-sor project at MiniComputer Inc., and tried to put on hold the futile quest for my old self. But I knew that a taste of memory was as close as the JFO airport in neighboring New York, and at irregular inter-vals—every few months or so—I would drive there, alone, for a visit to my prior life, which lived in a sort of limbo in the Air Sahelia ter-minal. I began to make these trips every Friday night, like a weekend heroin addict driving into the city for his fix.

And like the addict, the compulsive masturbator, I would be stupified for hours afterwords, unsure of where I was or what I was doing, and after arriving home the next morning and kicking in the door and fucking that wife of mine who would be waiting there in her sheer teddy and red high heels. Like a lot of readers of your magazine I thought the stories were made up until what happened to me one night, and I fucked her and fucked her, and she had that devilish look in her eye that I could just make out above her nipple on her softball-sized breast, `reset`, and I took a walk in the woods across the street.

It was on just such a Saturday morning, fresh back from the airport and its magazines and memories, that I met Sister Anne Adair, the last of the New Kent Shakers.

I was given permission to, I mean I was walking through the woods, near the lake when I came upon a trail, barely discernable, that veered off through the underbrush. On a whim I followed it. It meandered through a meadow—faint, nearly gone; at times I thought I had lost it, or had confused it where deer trails crossed it. But every ten yards or so along this one faint trail there could be seen, if one looked closely enough, large flat stones, too regularly spaced to be merely providential: somebody had placed them there, like comments in the code, like breadcrumbs to mark the trail. Eventually I came upon an old stone fence.

Now, finding an old stone fence in the woods of a New England state like Vermont or New Kent is no wise an unusual occurrence: the woods are full of them. But this one was like none I had ever seen, so regular its construction, so elegant the placement of each stone. Soon I came upon a large rectangular arrangement of stones which I knew at once to be the foundation of a barn long gone. A barn built with more than precision and craftsmanship: a barn resplendent with love in each of its foundation stones.

Close thereby were houses which in their dilapidation still plainly showed the austere yet somehow joyous lines of their design. I felt, in coming upon this empty village, like a boy-explorer imagining himself in an ancient castle, whose queen, with breasts the size of softballs, is imprisoned in the tower, and I was surprised to see the faintest wisp of smoke coming from the chimney of a small white house. As I stood there, amazed, a door opened and a short, ancient but visibly spry woman stepped out. I felt like Hansel coming upon the gingerbread house, unsure whether it boded good or ill. She motioned for me to go to her, and I did.

There are different ways we communicate, we humans, whether by words, touch, facial expression, pictures drawn in the sand, pheromones, electrolytes, antennae, TCP/IP, dance, or the simple gesture of a shared bit of honey.
RETURN.

It was at this point that Dr. Witold looked up from the bag of bottles and cans that he was sorting, and, pretending to be bored

with the incredible story I had just told him, said, with a most therapeutic mock-severity: "What the fuck is wrong with your nose?"

Indeed there was something wrong with my nose: it was red
and swollen and the bee stinger was still lodged in it, giving the
impression of a cross between an inflamed pimple and a hairy mole.
I had been ignoring the stinger for the simple reason that the more
my nose throbbed the more my penis did as well, and I found it increasingly pleasurable. But with his few simple words Dr. Witold had
brought home to me the necessity of facing up to the facts: I had a
bee stinger in my nose, and it was time to do something about it.
"Excuse me," I said. "Let me take care of it, then I can finish telling you about Anne Adair and the Shaker village of Simplicity. You
will find her story every bit as astounding as that of my return from
Sahelia, and my evanescent location-sensitive memory."

"I don't give a fuck what you do. Why don't you leave me
alone?" were his only words, and I appreciated the ironic double
meaning, his subtle way of providing therapy even while engaging in
the role of "friend."

"Excuse me, Doctor," I said, "would you point me towards
your bathroom, please?"

"Use outside," he said, pretending not to take my meaning, "I
hate these fucking cans with no deposit."

Dr. Witold was being deliberately obtuse: obviously it was
the bathroom mirror that I was interested in, not the 'facilities;' yet
not being an expert in Polish manners, I pretended to go along with
him, and left by the front door. After all, it was no more than a few
hundred yards from his front porch to my house. I could go home,
take care of the stinger (not to mention taking care of my wife, which,
I must tell you, every time I kick in that door, she's got to have it),
and be back with my friend Dr. Witold in a matter of minutes.

Upon leaving his house and turning down the tree-lined road
towards my humble house (which, I am perfectly willing to admit,
looked more like an abandoned nut-house residence than the private
home of a highly compensated computer designer; I simply had not
had the time or cash to fix it up yet), I noticed a new species of
flower, and I'm sure that you know the ones I'm thinking of; they are
blue and hang like bonnets from a vertical stem. They hadn't been
there the week before. Curiously, however, the once-green lawn in
front of the greenhouse was now a pasty white, and full of mother-
fucking clover.

I went home, kicked in the door; some potassium would help. I can feel it.

I went home, kicked in the door, my wife was there, her sweet softball breasts fairly spilling out of her white 'miracle' brassiere; she, a brilliant physicist, was working on a new form of 'lukewarm' fusion, but as soon as she saw me, well, you can just imagine. Do not reset.

CONTINUE.

I went into the bathroom.

CONTINUE.

I went into the bathroom, where her brassieres were drying: white, red, black.

CONTINUE.

That had so recently held those magnificent softballs.

CONTINUE.

I pulled that ol' stinger. I grabbed that ol' hand lotion, the moisturizing kind with the perfume that smells somehow of clover, I mean wildflowers, so soft and white to the touch, and I grabbed that stinger, and I pulled it; it hurt; then I pushed it, it felt better; I pulled it, it hurt; I pushed, better; pulled, hurt, pushed, better, pulled, pushed, pulled, pushed, pulled, pushed, Reset. Pushpullpush-pull. Reset. Puplpplpllppppppppp. Reset. RESET. RESET!!!!

This is the tale of how I lost my concentration, and how I got it back. It does not purport to be pretty.

The story of my confusion has everything to do with a simple logical error in the design of a floating point processor, the number-processing part of a computer that deals with decimal numbers. I repeat: my confusion was caused by a design bug, the kind of bug that is vexingly hard to find but, once found, simple to fix.

I was going to debug Kali or die trying. Kali was a floating point chip. Whoever said that Kali was a cache-controller was pulling your leg.

But anyway, I found that beastly bug. After noodling on a guitar for a little while I realized that I was, at last, sleepy. I was, in fact, utterly exhausted. I put the guitar down and staggered up the stairs to my first-floor bedroom. The window was open and there was a pile of snow on the floor. I went over and lifted the sash another inch or two. A gust pushed the curtains up and snow blew into the room. Perfect, I thought. A beautiful woman, my wife. I sat on the edge of my mattress and jotted a few notes in my work diary, then toppled over, pulled the rumpled quilt over my sweaty body, and was instantly unconscious.

You may find it odd that such a simple thing as a floating point error could have driven me to such distraction, to the point that I wondered whether I should check myself into the nearly-empty facility across the street from my house for some two thousand fucking volts across the cranium; I mean, to set my wits to rights. However, if I were to remind you of how the search for understanding, or truth, or the philosopher's stone had driven countless philosophers and saints to apparent madness, you would say, "Of course. The search for truth always incurs the risk of madness."

Maybe the problem, then, lies in your not understanding enough about floating point performance, and the class of problem to which it pertains. So perhaps now, before returning to Dr. Witold in his residence along the Potemkin path (where we will tell him the story of Simplicity, the Shaker village), we should take a little detour through the world of the simplex algorithm, linear programming, floating point boards, the fate of our poor human species, and so forth (without getting ahead of ourselves and talking about C-Transfer, an altogether different thing). Yes, I have made up my mind: that is what we shall do. We shall eddy here in the appendix of exposition while our story proper flows by above, languorously, in the great intestine of narrative flow, where we shall catch up with it anon. Is that all right with you, Betsy? Is it alright if we take a little detour through some computational theory before rejoining the story? No? You would prefer that I get right back on track without any such detour? You would rather that I skip the boring stuff, and get right back to Dr. Witold? Is that what you would like?

No. Alas, it cannot be so.

But I assure you, it is important. It is important, as you listen to this little tale of a forgotten Shaker village hidden on a nut-house estate, to follow with me as I tell of things mathematical and technological. The topics are dense, but not overly so, and you have the brains to follow the discussion, and you must, or your time is wasted. Because I tell you that I am in earnest, in life and death earnest, and so are you, who are giving your day, or night, to be with me. This hour that you spend with me, you will not see it again. It is one hour gone on your way to the grave. So spend it well. Pay attention.

Now you will be saying to yourself: 'The voice is not right. This is not fun any more.' Paavo has slipped out of character.' But do not be so smug. We all see the story-telling glitch, the little slip-up, the stage fright. All of us see it, whether we be a sophisticate in an airplane at thirty-thousand feet or a humble peasant squatting in the Sahelian dust. We are all human beings, and we all see the sun rise and set. So do not tell me, as you laugh at my lapses, that *your* pain is not real. It *is* real. I feel it as you feel it. I am with you. And I will be with you, always.

Linear programming, having been invented and put into practice some years before the first digital computer felt the first electron coursing through its soulless brain, is not intrinsically related to the programming of an analytical engine. Linear programming is a mathematical technique for modeling reality, a way of maximizing a function of a finite number of dependent variables subject to a set of inequalities. Linear programming can be speeded up with a computer, but it can be done with a pencil and a sheet of paper. Don't be put off, Betsy, this is not so abstract as it sounds. In fact it is palpably physical, as real as anything you might hold in your own sweet hand, or nestle ever so gently into a lacy bit of underclothing.

Let's illustrate by example. Say that you wanted to maximize the value of the output of your farm, a nice little farm in northern New Kent, with a lovely view of Lake Venzig. How would we use a linear programming model to do this? Well, the *objective function* that you were trying to maximize would be profit, which we can approximate by cash that you could get from the sale of your farm's output, such as corn, or wheat, or soybeans or milk. The more you sell, of course, the more cash you take in, and the more things you buy, such as fertilizer, and seeds, and tractors, well obviously that would take away from profits. The *inequalities* would simply state that you had to use an amount of land that was less than or equal to what you had, and an amount of fertilizer that was less than or equal to what you had, and so forth. And you would build a big mathematical description of your farm, with prices, yields, costs, all elegantly stated. So you can see how it goes. And Mr. Danzig, he invented a mathematical way of determining the best way to get the most money out of the farm, and he called it simplex, and it goes like this: in iterations. You put in a starting guess of how you plan to use your resources, and you turn the mathematical crank, as if you were cranking a gramophone, and the algorithm gives you a better guess, an improvement. And then you do it again. Each iteration is a solution, a way to farm the farm: forget the soybeans, the solution says; go with corn. And so on.

Danzig's method guarantees that, in almost every case, each iteration gives a better solution than the one before it. So eventually you get to the very best way to farm the farm. This is called convergence. And that is what we are all seeking. Convergence.

But here is a warning: do not put a mathematical description of your bees, your apiary, into the model. For some things have souls, and even to try to quantify them is in itself an act of blasphemy. Some things must be felt by the soul, not measured by the eye. Some things—like the precise degree of a refugee child's longing for her home, which is gone, or the degree of breathlessness I experience in contemplating the angle of your neck—cannot be quantified. Do not try. It is blasphemy.

Now in the days of the Second World War, when Moloch, all that which is most vile within us, was animating the German people, there was a great need for mathematicians to help with the business of supplying the troops who were fighting so bravely to put Moloch back in its foul dungeon. You have only to imagine that you were quartermaster to the allied armies to see why this was so.

Danzig used his algorithm to help find the best way to supply the troops. But he had no computer to turn the mathematical crank for him. He had instead a small army of humans, each of whom had a simple mechanical calculator, and that was how they did it.

Nowadays we have computers to do the calculations for us. And the parts of the computer that work on numbers are the floating point processor and the array processor. So you see where we are, don't you, sweetness? You understand me, Betsy? But Betsy, why am I talking to you in this way? It was you after all, wasn't it, who took over the management of the FP project after I was re-assigned to write the manual!

The fight against Moloch is ever so much more demanding these days than it was in 1943. We can no longer turn the crank by hand and expect to prevail. Moloch has upgraded his skills and so must we. We need computer assistance. Moloch is in our cities, feeding crack to our children. Moloch is in Africa, using slaves to steal gold from the ground. Moloch is on the television, selling us the lie that selfishness is our chiefest virtue. Moloch... But enough about Moloch. He does not exist. I was speaking metaphorically.

    With a good floating point processor you can work the numbers. You can square the circle, reconcile that which is irreconcilable. This was my fundamental insight. Others might have seen the processor as a simple "number cruncher," but I, upon reading those books in the empty halls of JFO Airport, with my ability to see deep deep patterns (somehow enhanced, I believe, by the Zen-like void that occupied my mind at that time, when my Freemerican identity was beyond my ken, and my Sahelian identity of 'Ntrang 'Nkoolan was in hiding, overcome) I saw immediately what no one before me had been able to see: with a powerful enough floating point processor we could solve the biggest resource allocation problem of all: the allocation of wealth and health and justice among the people of the world. I wanted to build a processor that could teach us how best to farm the earth, to feed the children, to eliminate hate and misunderstanding, to stop unwanted sexual advances.[6]

    This sounds more crazy than it is (as flying machines sounded crazy in the years before Orville and Wilbur). That is why I was so happy when Tom Best showed that film at Woodstock. It was his way of saying that I am not crazy. Despite my poor way with words, I am certain that I could explain it to you. But rather than belabor the point here, let us resume the narrative. Understanding will come with time. The seed has been planted; let it take root. This is what Jesus said.

    As soon as I had removed the stinger (with my nose and penis still both throbbing, but the pleasure and pain precisely canceling each other out) I walked back up the hill to see my dear friend Dr. Witold. In my absence he had prepared for me a delightful concoction, somewhat reminiscent of the taste of the nectar of that flower that brewers use in making beer.[7] "What is this delightful drink?" I asked, as I took my seat on his divan, a fanciful construction of baled newspapers.

---

[6] Or to clarify the meaning of innocent offers that might have been misunderstood as unwanted sexual advances.

[7] I will think of the name of this flower in a moment. It starts with the letter "H".

"Pisswater, what do you think it is," he said jocularly, and then, as a tease, made a dumb-show of pretending to empty the contents of a rusted can into my glass.

"Oh now, come on, none of that," I said. "Listen, and I will tell you about Simplicity."

"I ain't going to stop you," he said, and went back to his bottles and cans, which I took to be his signal to go on. And this is what I told him, which, at the time, was all that I knew about Simplicity. At the time, that is to say, I had not unraveled the central mystery of that forlorn yet somehow joyous ghost-village in the woods.

"Simplicity was a religious working community," I began, "a full-fledged member village of the United Society of Believers in the First and Second Appearing of Christ, who were known to the World, and to themselves, as Shakers. It was founded under the auspices of the Elders and Eldresses of the Church; that is, the parent Family, at New Lebanon, New York in 1813, between the founding of the Union Village (Ohio) and Watervliet (Ohio) communities, which are generally reckoned to be the fourteenth and fifteenth of the nineteen acknowledged Shaker churches. The founding Family, consisting of twelve Brothers and Sisters from the New Lebanon, Harvard (Massachusetts), South Union (Kentucky) and Sabbathday Lake (Maine) Churches arrived in Eastboro on April fourth and, with Brother Ephraim and Sister Lucy acting as trustees, took possession of the land (two thousand acres) that had been deeded to them by the prosperous and eccentric mercantile magnate Stanley Cohen, a Jew, who, estranged from his own heritage and contemptuous of conventional Christianity, saw in the Shakers something new under the sun, and good.

"Within five years the population of the village had grown to nearly three hundred souls, with a ratio of Brothers to Sisters of six to five. Like all Shaker communities, the people of Simplicity were largely self-sufficient, but they did purchase some wares from the World, including tin, glass, and iron; and in turn they sold to the World as well: furniture, cloth, and honey: sweet, sweet honey. Thus their buildings included (in addition to the usual Dwelling, Meeting House, school, barns and infirmary) a sawmill, linen mill ("loom"), furniture shop, and honey house. The Simplicity Shakers, being strictly celibate like all Shakers, grew in ranks by welcoming adult converts to the faith (some of whom joined as families, with children) and by adopting abandoned children, usually orphans, who were raised in the faith and often (but not always) chose to remain in it upon reaching the age of majority. The population of Simplicity remained about constant, fluctuating between two hundred and eighty-seven members and three hundred and fourteen members from 1818 until 1884.

In 1884, the year in which Sister Anne Adair was born, however, the population decreased drastically: from 314 to 112 members. Through the next century this number dwindled at an actuarial rate that more or less matched the decline of Shakers everywhere. In 1911 the twenty-one remaining Simplicity Shakers deeded their land to the state of New Kent for its state mental hospital, with the proviso that they (the Shakers) be left in peace as long as they lived. In 1963 Brother Hosea passed away, leaving Sister Anne to live alone for the next twenty years, which she was able to do quite comfortably, thanks to the boundless supply of provisions put up over the preceding century. Until I arrived at her doorstep on that day in 1984, the last person from the World that she had seen was the undertaker who had seen to the internment of Brother Hosea."

That was all there was to the story; I stopped and tried to guess what Dr. Witold's reaction would be.

Now, as presented, this story raises several intriguing questions: Why the drop in population in 1884? No other community had experienced anything like it. Why the deeding of the land to the State for a mental hospital? Why the total estrangement from the World? Other communities, in their twilight years, became more and more engaged with the World, not less. What had set Simplicity on such a different path?

At the time I did not mention to Dr. Witold the most curious fact of all: that the name of the New Kent Shaker village of Simplicity appeared nowhere in any history of the Shaker movement that I could find in the local library. I did not know then what I know now: that the village of Simplicity appears nowhere in any Shaker document whatsoever. As far as the United Society of Believers in the First and Second Appearing of Christ was concerned, the village of Simplicity had never existed.

I looked at my friend and mentor. "Well?" I said.

"Fucking bullshit!" Dr. Witold said. "I hate these cans with no fucking deposit!"

A floating point processor[8] is a wonderful thing, but it is not a universal computer, not a Turing Machine that can do anything and everything that a computer can do. It works on numbers in a very specific, well-defined format, as documented in the IEEE specification.[9] There are certain computer applications for which a floating point processor is simply not well suited. If, for example, one were to try to build a story-telling machine, one would want to steer clear of floating point processors altogether. A story-telling machine that was based on a floating point processor, even a bug-free floating point processor, would be bound to approach storytelling as if it were some kind of linear programming problem to be solved in iterations, always looping back on itself, dropping threads, skipping like a scratchy record, a CD that somebody has left in the rain; wrong but somehow plausible, like a bird in the water, or a fish in the air. And a *buggy* floating point processor? What kind of story could you write with one of *those*? You don't even want to hear about it.

Yet a resource-allocation program to distribute wealth, health and justice in the world—the kind of problem to which a floating point processor is perfectly well suited—would need a way to express itself, a way to convince people to change their Moloch-driven ways and pay attention to the truly important things: the greatness within us, and the good uses we could put our greatness to—finding a home for the child without a home, giving succor to the persecuted and the weak, providing hope to the wretched of the earth, and putting something good to eat, something very good to eat, such as an avocado—perhaps an avocado; not overripe—soft but not mushy—let's say two of them: two softball-sized avocadoes, a pair of honey-covered avocados—into the mouths of the truly, truly hungry.

That is what I was trying to tell Tom Best at Woodstock. If busty, leggy women and poisoned food had not derailed me I would have told him of my plan to link, over a memory bus, the FP and

---

[8] A working, bug-free floating point processor.

[9] Institute of Electronic and Electrical Engineers. Which specification, I should point out, was put together by a very political process, which had very little to do with efficient ways of storing numbers inside a digital computer, and very much to do with the relative clout of certain computer-industry giants, which shall, for now, remain nameless, whose designated members to the committee wouldn't know an elegant solution to underflow problems if it bit them in the ___ as they stood in their clover-filled lawns in Bellevue, Washington.

the NLP (natural language processor) that Shareena was working on. The memory bus is an important part of the architecture. It would have worked, too, had not the bureaucrats at MiniComputer sent me packing. I just needed to do a little more research. Anyway that was the state of my thinking about these matters in those idle weeks after I left MiniComputer, Inc. and before I joined Zeus (with a gracious recommendation from Tom Best himself) as Director of Floating Point Operations.

It was on one of those idle days, three weeks into my unemployment (two months after meeting Dr. Witold, six months after the curious conversation with the resurrectionist angel in the woods), that I learned of the colloquium entitled "Computational Aspects of Consciousness" to be held at the University of New Kent upon Thursday of the week following. I had just returned from my morning visit to Sister Anne, when, arriving at my mailbox at the same time as the mailman and my wife (who was wearing short-shorts and a halter top that left little to the imagination—mine or the smiling mailman's), I found the announcement, curiously addressed to "Resident."

It had become my practice to go see Sister Anne every morning. She, having spent twenty years alone after the death of Brother Hosea, was happy for company. Not desperate for company, I hasten to add. She was not an unhappy woman, and solitude did not distress her. But at the age of one hundred years, she was the last of her family, the last of her way of life, the last keeper of the knowledge of Simplicity—and she was happy to have me come to call. We would meet in her modest, elegant kitchen for herb tea, jam, and biscuits—just as you, Betsy, might go to visit your grandmother, in her walk-up flat in West Orange. The herbs for the tea had been harvested and dried a half a century before; the jam and the mix from which she baked the biscuits were not quite so old, but nearly; but they tasted like heaven. The kindling and firewood for her stove had been put up by Brother Hosea. It was as if two centuries of careful preparation for the future had been consummated in the life of Sister Anne Adair.

At first our conversations had been merely conventional, full of pleasantries about the weather, the beauty of the forest, and so forth. But over time she began to tell me of her life in the village in the old days: the daily rituals of work and worship "putting hands to work and hearts to God," the rhythm of the farm, the personalities of her Brothers and Sisters. I was enthralled; simply being in her company seemed to set my electrolytic balance just right. Within days of our having met, I had become something of a student of the history of the Shakers, to the extent that I had read everything available at the local library.

I never mentioned to Sister Anne my discovery of the curious absence of Simplicity from all records of Shakerism. There would have been no point in that. But clearly there was a mystery there, and it began to nag at me. One morning, on about my tenth visit, she said, "Come, Paavo, I have something that I would like to show you." I followed her down the clean, bright hallway—clear and spare, as every Shaker design—to a varnished wooden door. "Here you will find our records," she said, and pushed the handle.

The door opened upon a room containing no furniture other than a desk and chair, and on the desk was a single book. Along the walls were built-in drawers and shelves with boxes neatly stacked, and incredibly, dust free. "Our sales and purchases," she said. "Our roster, with additions to our Family, and our deaths. Our plantings and harvests. Our letters and journals. All of our records are here. You may read them, but they must never leave this room. Except for the book," she said, pointing to the volume on the desk. "That is for you."

It was on the morning of that same Thursday, that same short-short, halter-top Thursday, that I asked Sister Anne whether she knew any reason for the precipitous decline in the village's population in the year 1884.

At first I thought that she had not heard me. She looked at me closely, and slowly, ever so slowly, a smile appeared at the corners of her mouth. Before that very minute, despite our weeks of friendship, I had never seen her smile. You understand, she was spry, but she was old; one hundred years old, and very wrinkled. She wore the Shaker bonnet, and a black dress of coarse cloth. She was tiny. Her shoes were hand-stitched. Everything in her kitchen had been made by hand. You must imagine this, if you wish to properly imagine the impact of her tiny smile upon my jaded, polar-amnesiac soul. The Shakers were emphatic about light and fresh air: at a time when the Victorians had been draping rooms in layer upon layer of brocade and velvet, filling every crack to stop the 'draughts,' the Shakers filled their rooms with light from uncurtained windows kept open wide. The study, that day, was brilliant.

Finally she sang this hymn, in her high, almost bee-like voice, a hymn that I have only heard sung that one time:

More love! More love! The heavens are blessing
The angels are calling, O Zion, more love
If ye love not each other in daily communion
How can ye love God, whom ye have not seen?
If ye love one another then God dwelleth in you
And ye are made strong to live by his word
More love! More love! Alone by its power
The world we will conquer, for true love is God

You might have supposed that news of the colloquium—about as far from old ladies in the woods as you can get—would have dislodged Sister Anne from my mind, but the evocative words of that hymn were the very words that were sounding in my ears, pianissimo, as I ran up the street, with the flyer in my hand and an erection of considerable size and rigidity straining against my zipper, towards the home of my guru, Dr. Witold. Little did I know that those words spoken to me by Sister Anne were not only to be her last to me on that halter-busting Thursday, but her last words ever on this earth.

Looking back from the vantage of more than fifteen years, I can still feel the excitement that I felt that busty mid-morning. Morning, as I raced up to tell Dr. Witold of the colloquium. And if I was excited then, I am all the more so now, for that colloquium was to be the turning point of my life, and the architecture of my memory is such that reliving past moments of extreme electrolytic activity evokes a similar response now, only amplified. Although I could not have known it as I ran, hard, up the Potemkin path, I was destined not only to meet, but to cross-fertilize (I am speaking metaphorically) with the people I would meet—Marvin Kinsky, David Hoofstatle, and Manuel Benet—the fathers of the entire consciousness transfer movement.

Kinskey, who looked a little like a bald Ringo Starr. Hoofstatle, whose voice, when speaking of subjects about which he felt most closely, had a delightfully round timbre, not unlike Paul McCartney's. Bennet, the twinkle in whose eye oddly enough reminded me of the photo of George Harrison on the cover of the *Let It Be* album. The undergraduate women at the doors to the lecture hall on the University of New Kent campus, like so many apple scruffs, waiting for a chance to satisfy their idols, of whom I was to become one. Dr. Witold and his cans. My wife, the softballs. The undergraduate women in their white white lacy panties. Consciousness, the floating point architecture. The avocados carried on plates by the undergraduate women in their lacy brassieres, some more full than others; some shy, some bold, like an eraser. Many flowers. Pushpins. Reset. Satisfying their idols. Stinger. Push, pull. Reset. Their lacy white avocadoes. Softballs. Clover field. Reset. My wife and the smiling mailman, nothing to the imagination. Reset. Reset. Gatorade. The undergraduate women by the door, waiting for Hoofstatle to speak, with her calves, right around left, left around right, his head nestled. Reset. Gatorade. About a gallon. Internet. Namby pamby. Reset. Memory architecture, the breasts fairly spilling out of her red softballs. Gatorade, reset. I emptied about. Reset. About a gallon of jism all over her breasts, and she loved every drop. Gatorade. I emptied. Gator. Rese. RRRR.

Let me ask you something, friends. Have you seen our new information piece featuring the Starshine automobile?

Oh No! Some moron put in the solder flux. Turn off the radio! Gatorade, Quick!!

You know the one I'm talking about, with the Statue of Liberty bending down to pick up one of those nice bright new cars from the ferry to Manhattan. Yeah, you've seen it? Isn't it great? It's a great prodvert. I gotta tell you, I love it, I love it myself... Wait a minute, John's shaking 'no'. You folks listening on radio instead of watching on the 'net can't see this, but our producer, John, is shaking his head no. He hasn't seen the ad. I can't believe it. Come on. Really?

He's saying really.

(□ □)

That sound you just heard is me being speechless. That's the way I laugh when I'm speechless—which you regular listeners know doesn't happen very often, me being speechless. But my producer, John, has made me speechless. The man has no shame, ladies and gentlemen, no shame. My own producer. Well that just goes to show you, you can't control everything. Your own producer hasn't even seen the most talked about prodvert in all television and webspace combined. I tell you, that's why I love this job: surprises. Surprises every day: John has not seen the Starshine prodvert. John, haven't you plugged in? Anybody who watches any television at all has seen this piece. I'm not talking about being glued to the set, spending your whole life there, I'm talking about watching the telescreen as little as six hours a day. If John had either watched TS or plugged into the net as little as six hours a day there is no way he could have missed that information-sharing piece by now. Even on the kind of channels that I'm sure John tunes into in his leisure time—heh heh, you catch my drift, I'm sure. John's a male, for you who haven't guessed. Drone, through and through. Does that give you an idea of the kind of channel he likes? But hey, what am I talking about? I better change the topic, this is a family program! There are larvae out there listening!

Jesus Christ, who put in the solder flux? For the love of God, get me some Gatorade.

In a way I'm glad, though, because it gives me the opportunity to make an important point: you can't control everything. That's an important point, let me say it again: you cannot, that's N-O-T not, control everything. Don't try telling that to a non-bee. Or to a honeybee, for that matter.

Gatorade. Please. Gatorade.

Glad to be here. We'll be back to our topic in a minute, but first we have to pay some bills. We do that by selling advertising space, and we're not ashamed to admit it. This is not National Public Radio. We're not going to come begging to you for money every two minutes or stealing your tax dollars to pay for this program. Instead we're going to give our sponsors an opportunity to speak to you, through me. Simple as that. Bee enterprise. We're proud of it. It's what put Freemerica on the map.

You know what I'm going to talk about, right? You bet you do! Clover. Clover industries, our proud sponsor. And here's the message: you pick up the pollen, bring

it back to the hive. Clover industries pays you. What could be more simple? If you're a humble bee that's what you do. Why? Why do we do this, you ask? Let's all give the answer together: Because we love our children is why, obviously! Of course the non-bees and honeybees don't want to hear you say that, do they? Noooooo. Seems like the non-bees have got a monopoly on parental caring. The non-bees are so caring, so compassionate. Just listen to them, they'll tell you! They don't want to admit that maybe humble bees care about their children too. They say we collect clover not because we're compassionate people, but because we like to get stuff. That's your crime, ladies and gentlemen: you like to get stuff. What kind of stuff? How about cars, jet-skis, nights on the town, sex, can openers, tequila, inkjet printers, sex, hair transplants, brass buttons, sex, petroleum, cocaine, baskets, telephones, cameras, camcorders, jumbo jets, metal detectors, flack jackets, surface-to-air missiles, Disney animated movies on videocassettes, mace, pepper spray, magazine clips, hand grenades, sex, and food for our kids. As if there were anything wrong with wanting those things in the first place! But that's what the liberals, I mean non-bees, accuse us of. Wanting food for our kids. If that's the crime I'm accused of, I guess you can call me guilty.

Gatorade or pull my plug.

Am I missing something? Is there something <u>wrong</u> with wanting food for our children? If there are any of you non-bees listening out there, please give us a call and explain

to us why it's so wrong to want to feed our children. I must be stupid, I guess. I just don't get it. Meanwhile all you humble bees out there, collect pollen and get stuff. Joyously partake of this wonderful bee enterprise system, the wonder of the world. OK that's the end of this ad.

Now let's get back to that Starshine prodvert I was telling you about. If John hasn't seen it, I'm going to have to assume some of you haven't out there in cybeespace haven't seen it yet either, so let me describe it to you. This is what I'm going to do: I'm going to describe it to you, then I'm going to tell you what the non-bees don't like about it, and then I'm going to explain to you why they're wrong.

Start by imagining the Statue of Liberty standing tall and green and proud out there in New York harbor. I gotta tell you, I can look out my studio window right now and see Miss Liberty, and she is one beautiful lady. When I think of what she means to the world, and what the non-bees say about her...

Sorry, I got a little choked up there for a minute. I'm alright, just let me take another sip of nectar here... There, that's better. Nothing like a little sip of clover nectar when you're feeling choked up.

Gatorade.

The Starshine prodvert starts with a closeup of Miss Liberty's face—the sculptor, by

the way, used his own mother's face for a model—no end to the facts you'll learn if you stay tuned—and then the camera pans down from her face to the harbor below, where a ferry, you know, those Staten Island ferries? A ferry is passing by with some automobiles on the open deck, and there's one particular auto that catches Miss Liberty's eye, and that's the Starshine. Well she just bends down and she picks it up, ever so gently, and she holds it in the palm of her hand, like a loving heavenly beekeeper might... This is choking me up, ladies and gentlemen... and she just looks at that automobile, and

you can see that Freemerican
pride starting to beam out of
her face, and she puts it down
on the ferry and stands back
up, with her torch held high,
and a smile on her face, and
the music is playing that old
Christian hymn

'Tis God's gift to be
wealthy

'Tis God's gift to be me

'Tis God's gift to drive
where 'ere I want to be...

Now anybody can see the
beauty of this prodvert. What
does it tell us? One: that the
Starshine is a luxury car, that
people who have been blessed
by God should be happy to
drive it. Two: that the Statue of

Liberty, who stands for nothing if not the free flow of capital to world markets, likes this
car, and the wealth-creating
trade it represents. That's it.
Excellent product, excellent
message: excellent prodvert.
No wonder the non-bees hate
it so much.

Gatorade.

Now, if you listen to the
non-bees, and the honey-
bees, this is what they are
going to tell you are the
words on the base of the
Statue of Liberty: "Give me
your tired, your hungry,
your poor, your huddled
masses yearning to breathe
free, the wretched refuse of
your teeming shore." Now

before I comment on that, let's talk for a minute about Chief Seattle. You remember this one, don't you? This speech that became the anthem of the watermelons— that's what some people call environmentalists, green on the outside, pink on the inside—watermelons? It was supposedly the pious words of Chief Seattle, the indigenous Freemerican chief who soooo loved the earth? You remember, how it turned out to be all made up by one of their speech writers in Houston?

Gatorade.

Guess what. They did it again. They did it again,

Ladies and gentlemen, and this is so important to clear up that I'm going to do something unprecedented in the annals of Excellence in Pheromone Communication. I'm going to skip the prodvert break that we have scheduled here, when I would normally break to make a mention of Billy Beer, and a damn fine beer it is too, but I think the folks at Billy Beer would not object, given the importance of what I'm in the middle of explaining here, to my neglecting to mention Billy Beer, that great-

tasting stuff. Because some things, like our great Freemerican traditions are more important than individual products, even great Freemerican products like Billy Beer, and the folks at Billy Beer, great patriotic Freemericans that they are, will forgive me this one time, this only time that I'm going to skip right over the prodvert so we don't lose momentum.

"Tell us Ralph," you're saying. "What did they do again?" Well, I'll tell you what. I sent my fact checkers over to see the

Statue of Liberty, see it with their own eyes. Guess what they found out.

Do you want to know what it really says on the Statue of Liberty?

Are you ready?

Four letters: RSVP.

Gatorade.

Ladies and gentlemen, I have in my studio with me today Rosie Krahammar, the famous author of "Since the Venzig Wall Came Down."

Rosie, you're a cultured lady. Can you tell our friends out there in pheromone land what those four letters stand for?

Oh sure I can. You know I can, Ralph. They stand for Répondez S'il Vous Plâit

Which means...?

Dat means you are supposed to let people know in advance that you are coming. But of course you cannot RSVP without you have an invitation. Now anybody with any educaytion at all knows that. Only people who were raised in a bahn or something do not know 'RSVP'. I don't mean Freemericans of course if dey don't know what dot means. Freemericans are the ones what have built all the wealth; of course some of them don't have time to go to learn French. But what I mean is like these Africans that you see stahving all the time. They are the ones what don't like to work, so you would think that they would have some time to learn French or some manners anyway...

And how would one go about getting an invitation to come to Freemerica, if one happened to be of the overseas branch of the hive?

Oh dot is very easy, Ralph. You have only to call this man in Alexandria Virginia at World Relations, what is wot dey call a consulting firm, you know. You have only to tell them that you want a green card, a permanent visa to this country, and they will tell you what companies you can buy, you have only to spend maybe one or two million dollars, and then you own dat company, which is still a Freemerican company

# of course, even dough you own it, so now you can come over any time you like, for to take care of your company...

Gatorade.

This routine issues the ARM command to the specified clock. This routine places the clock in bypass mode and sets up the clock chip in an appropriate fashion. This routine reads the current threshold set by the specified Digital/Analog converter, and returns it as a floating point number, in volts. This routine sets the threshold on the specified D/A converter to a specified voltage. It internally performs the read/modify/write operation necessary. This routine issues the DISARM command to the specified clock. This routine enables or disables the interrupt gate on the CK10 corresponding to the specified channel. This can be used to generate interrupts for modules that do not have this ability. The microcode must clear the done bit before re-enabling interrupt unless mrwion is used. This routine should not be used for a CK10 in any slot other than slot C, except for the 'internal' clocks (y and z). This routine does not affect the clocks directly. It merely identifies which clock will be used with a particular transfer. When the transfer is initiated, these clocks will be disarmed, device setups will be performed, then the clocks will be re-armed. Clocks may also be specified as arguments to some transfer routines, and will behave the same way as if they had been identified by mrclktrig. When mropen is used for a clock, it opens the clock in bus-window mode so that other routines need not open and close bus-window mode repeatedly. This routine will convert an input start pulse or level to a level suitable for gating other clocks on and off. This routine is only mentioned because it is used with mrclkintgat and mrwnion, though it does nothing special in the case of the CK10.

There is no room they can go to, and yet they must. God is upon them, the Holy Spirit. They would sooner die than offend their brethren or sistren, yet at the same time they must meet, or die. Where?

"Sister," says he. "I must go now, to replace the implements in the barn. Tonight will be a full moon, and there, I suppose, about the second hour, the moonlight will shine through the window above the western door onto the hayloft. Now I must be off, Sister. Until we meet again, farewell."

"Farewell to thee, Brother," she answers, hoping, with no good reason to hope, that her cheeks are not flushing crimson. Hoping, with no good reason to hope, that when the moon is full, at midnight, she will lose her courage, or her will, or her wakefulness, and pass to sleep on the harsh staw mattress whereupon she has slept for eighteen years, ever since her arrival here at the age of ten.

No avail. The moon shines in her eyes as bright as any noon. She slips her feet to the floor (she wore her dress to bed; none saw), barely sitting upright as she does. Now she stands. Eleven minutes, by her pulse, from first toe on the floor until she is fully erect. She cannot tell whether the air be warm or cold: her body is neither, having gone into a realm beyond temperature, consisting of pure fear and anticipation. Her flesh contracts as in the coldest winter; her face is hotter than the sun. Between her legs there is a rivulet; her undergarment is coarse, now wet, as if she had sat upon the dew. She wonders whether she has wet her bed. No: this must be that other moisture.

He lies upon the hay, facing upward. He has loosend his garments, and now, for the first time in his forty-one years, he permits his right hand to touch: first his scrotum, so tight it might have been a change purse filled with coin; the hair thick and knotted. There is the faint aroma of a scented candle in the air. Whether it be rosewood or sandalwood, he does not care.

What is a narrative for our times? Race conditions. A crazy man turned into the authorities by his brother. Murdering people to call attention to the perceived threat of "technology." For example: CT scans that show enlarged ventricles, indicative of schizophrenia. If you mean that there exists the possibility for misuse of this technology, certainly you are right. But that is true of any science, of any technology. Steel can be used to make surgeon's scalpels or, what do you call them, dum-dum bullets.[10] Fertilizer can be used to grow crops or to make terrorist bombs. Computers can be used to explore the ocean bottom or to manipulate the stock market. It is up to society to determine how technology is put to use, not up to the scientist. A software mogul, the richest man in the world, might fund nanomachines to rearrange arbitrary sequences of DNA, their meanings clearly spelled out by the Human Genome Project. That is a narrative for our times.

> *Question:* What does it mean to be as little children? How are we to be as little children?
>
> *Answer:* We are to listen to the story. Children are willing story-listeners.

REM: Tom says this is OK let's let it keep running.

"Where can you get some fucking grub around here? Ain't there nothing up in them big brick buildings up there?" Dr. Witold said, in his inimical playful way. By this question I knew that he was inviting me to ride with him in his Pinto the scant quarter of a mile from his house to the main buildings atop the hill.

"You drive," he said. "I don't know how."

This seemed the best chance yet to tell him how I planned to save the world with numerical calculations, floating point numbers multiplied in vast arrays, technologically solving our problems. So, as soon as he got into the car I began my explanation:

"To begin with, the basic organization of all array processors is the same: some amount of on-board memory with some number of adders and multipliers and address generators all running in parallel. If you were simulating the activities in a human brain, for example, you would want to have considerable control of the arithmetic and address units in order to write efficient code for that particular application. You would need a special compiler for the machine.

---

[10] Actually they're made out of lead.

"With that compiler, the highly parallel architecture of the array processor becomes under Betsy's skillful manipulation a 'general purpose' high performance pipelined processor that just happens to be good at vector operations also. On the other hand, in signal processing, let's say, if you were taking somebody's brain waves and conditioning them, as a guitarist might do to the analog signals from his Stratocaster at an outdoor music festival, you would use a small set of highly optimized microcoded libraries for the basic operations. The large data sets involved would make the overhead of invoking an array processor 'small' relative to the compute time.

"Performing small sets of operations on large data sets allows for 'easy' partitioning of large problems so that when data transfer between host and AP is not prohibitive, only a small amount of AP memory is required for solving large problems—such as writing a novel, or removing injustice and want and pain from the world. It is worth noting, however, that some architectures do not provide the accuracy of 32-bit (longword) floating point; their designers have foolishly traded accuracy for speed, substituting16-bit (shortword) fixed points for the indicated floating points simply to save a few microseconds here or there. This temporal cost-cutting may lead to significant degredation in the brain's output—leading to an incomprehensible novel and some injustice.

"In the beginning was the word and the word was with God and the word was God. He was with God in the beginning. Through him all things were made; without him nothing was made that has been made. In him was life, and that life was the light of men. The light shines in the darkness, but the darkness comprehendeth it not. It is not clear from the spec whether this ur-word was a long word or a short word.

"I have sketched out the simulation and signal processing areas as if they were mutually exclusive. But most of what I said concerning simulation refers to very detailed large-scale simulation of the 'real world.' In mathematical modeling the solution of the problem usually reduces to solving a large and very sparse system of linear equations. These problems tend to be 'signal-processing like' in that they contain a small number of regular operations."

Dr. Witold really appreciated this explanation:

"Here I am on a sunny afternoon riding shotgun in a shitbox with the High Druid of Informationtology. Excuse me while I fling open the door and jump out under the wheels."

About bees and beehives and swarms:

Do not mistake the bee for the swarm. This is a reductionist error, the mistaking the part for the whole, otherwise known as the heresy of Schenectady. I mean senecdoche. I MEAN SYNECHDOCE. Fuckit. I do not know if I am a swarm, although I think I am not. I am in some ways like a drone. But I think I am more like a man. The simple truth is, I want to fuck. From the time I wake until the time I go to bed I want nothing more than to fuck, and at night, when I lay me down to sleep, I dream of fucking.

The novel moves from herky-jerky to fluidity, in iterations. It learns through back-propagation. Some approaches lead to dead ends. Some story lines we simply drop. So long, Anne Adair! The characters become progressively more real, less schematic. Light shows us Dr. Witold's patient sitting on chair, or a manuscript in an office above Broadway and 29th Street New York.

Chapter plot summaries. Code to be written. Partially complete scaffolding. Code commentary, arrays, pointers, indexed arrays, vectors into hash space. The dilapidated abandoned houses, the ghosts, the crazy man with the two women, the breaking glass, the watchman with the machete contrasted with the image I would rather have kept to myself: the little girl saying *"enna boubie"*, it's cold

The King of Zembla isn't dead. He's laid up, in a hospital, in a coma. Where his brain is hooked up to wires. That read brain waves. That are fed out over the Internet. And a Doctor. Is trying out drugs. And gene therapy. Microscopic machines adjust teleomeres. That are supposed to grow brain cells. Teleomeres. So that he can make sense of his memory, and reclaim his sanity. In the hospital Betsy visits him. Reads to him about Shakers and bees. And shows him porn movies of Honey Wilder, porn magazines about Betsy and Shareena.

Eternal life through teleomeres or through Jesus?

Above 29th Street, Manhattan, a literary agent is pondering what to do about this crazy fellow who has written these two novels. Note relating to people with mental illness. This could influence my story about the hospital & how it came to be there.

Father Murphy: "Gentlemen! What the hell is going on?"

Father Hessburg: "I hate Devotional Religion. But I love Sacramental Religion."

Once upon a time there was some discussion of whether users would ever be better off to load memory word by word rather than using direct memory access. For example, strides sufficiently large to place each vector element on a different page might be such a case. I plan to tell users how to load memory using MOVEs, but if there is no reason to load memory this way I can make the discussion terse. If on the other hand there is some kind of reasonable trade-off between DMA and word-by-word I need a better understanding of how to calculate the trade-off.

I need a better understanding of what the driver does when page translation is required so that I can explain how overheads may bear on algorithm design.

How else will I explain how Mary came to be here, in Eastboro? Under the current scheme, data pages must be locked in memory by the driver. Data that won't fit in memory must be segmented. How does user calculate cost of data segmenting? How do I make sense of my memories? The lust, the dust, the dying child?

Question: Do we know yet whether ASTs or Signals will be used?

Question: How does user specify another error handler?

Answer: OS will handle handshake with AP & signal asynchronously. User (library) will have access to (a) common block—to see what happened. (b) Ring Buffer to place continue or abort packet.

Question: What does Host/AP synchronization mean, and how is it implemented in the library?

Answer:

a) Poll field continuously;

b) Alternate sync'ing and polling;

c) Go to sleep and have system send wake-up when length field changes.

Question: What about loading co-efficient tables for FFTs?

Answer: The status word will contain record of interrupt-disabled exception; with interrupts disabled you'll have to check the word yourself to see if anything has gone wrong. Such as swallows at noon.

Question: How will user get access to this pointer?

Answer: When an exception happens, it seems that users should be able to branch on an exception, and reload the ring buffer, before issuing the CONTINUE statement. After all, the program has access to the RB to load the replacement opcode, so why can't the user load other packets while he's at it? Tom Best had an objection to this but I didn't understand it.

Question: How will I understand my coming to awareness?

Answer: The RB empty interrupt will get caught by the interrupt handler, which will send a signal, as usual. Race conditions may exist which make it impossible to tell which will get to the user first: the system call or the signal.

Question: How will I make any sense of my life?

Answer: In hallway conversation, Betsy argued for the operating system to figure it out. The argument is that RB empty is not an error, it's only a notice that something is done. The legs, the breasts, the heart-shaped asses. The necks, the turned-tooth smiles.

Question: How will I make any sense of my life?

Answer: Other conclusions about efficiency flow from this. Other voices have been heard to suggest that the signal handler should figure it out and leave the OS out of it.

What Mary said:

Unless you are as little children you shall not enter the kingdom of heaven, Jesus said, and he was right. So why do we try? We have no more chance of entering heaven than we have of fitting into the clothes we wore to sit on Grandmother's lap. Yet everywhere we strive, each in our own pathetic way, to become as little children: churchfuls of giants earnestly trying on dolls' dresses and sailor suits, hoping for a miraculous fit. I myself was once a child, until the day, when I was five years old, that I heard a man speak about the gospels. For me that was the beginning of the end.

At the Church of Our Lady in Bloomfield, New Jersey, the Holy Name Society convened for breakfast in the parish hall after the ten-thirty mass on a fine spring Sunday. While some men, including Lars, my grandfather, stood talking in small groups around the tables, other men wearing aprons were in the parish kitchen preparing scrambled eggs and sausage and rubbery white toast. I was not supposed to go in there but went anyway, laughing as I pushed open the swinging door. I should not even have been in the hall: the Society is a prayer group for adult men, and I was a five year old girl. Why was I allowed? I suppose it was because the men of the Society considered old Lars a kind of holy man, a man with a connection that they perhaps could use. Where Lars went, there went I, so if they wanted the connection they had to make allowances for me.

Lars, the old curmudgeon, had been sober for thirty years, but it wasn't until after his first heart attack that he found the Catholic God. Shortly after Lars's release from Bloomfield Hospital God spoke to him on the road from Belville to Newark, and after that the rosary was never far from his grease-stained hands, nor the words of the Hail Mary far from his tongue, which sixty years after his arrival at Ellis Island was still folded along its Swedish creases.

Lars was my grandfather; I ate my breakfast from his lap. I remember the parsley on the plate and the taste of the Wonder Bread soggy with butter. As we finished breakfast some priest spoke into a microphone, and the men all stood and muttered something, then the men all sat and I crawled under the table. Now another man stood up to a microphone, and everybody listened to him. I listened too; and that was when the eggshell of my childhood cracked.

I am sure that I misunderstood most of what the man said. It was grownup talk, boring and baffling, and it was also hard to hear from where I sat. But like a bee that knew just where I was hiding, his story sought me out and drove its stinger deep into my flesh.

He was a famous policeman who had just put a lot of bad people in jail, and the men all applauded him for that. Then he talked about the Jesus books. He said that he believed Matthew Mark Lukandjohn because they did not all say the same thing. If ten people saw the same thing they would all see it differently, he said, so if they all described it exactly the same it meant they were lying. But if they all described it a little differently then they were telling the truth. My five year old ears conveyed this message to my five-year-old brain, and I became upset. Suddenly the palisade of legs and shoes frightened me, and I crawled up on Lars's lap and buried my head in his Sunday jacket, confused about the Jesus books and wondering about truth.

Twenty-four years later I was still confused and wondering. I was by then a graduate student at Yale Divinity, on intimate terms with dozens of versions of the Jesus story. I was fluent in ancient Greek, Amharic and Ethiopic; conversant with the Dead Sea scrolls; able to debate the slightest doctrinal nuance separating Sadducee from Pharisee—or Pharisee from Essene or Maccabee. I myself had become a prosecutor of sorts: Jesus was on trial in the courtroom of my heart, and each ancient text had become a witness for me to interrogate. Like that untouchable New Jersey Mafia-buster I had heard at the Holy Name Society breakfast, I questioned each witness with a zeal bordering on the illegal. Unlike him, I could not find the truth in the witnesses' conflicting accounts, and the stinger remained lodged beneath my skin.

Which is not to say that I was a tortured soul; I was not. When Playboy came to campus recruiting for *Holy Cow! Women of the Divinity Schools* I was happy to pose naked before a roomful of men, and that laughter you see on my face (pages 87-88) is genuine. But even then I was seeking the truth; I was always seeking the truth, whether reading or praying or screwing or feeding the goldfish. But when the day came, when my prayers were answered and I stood upon Truth's threshold—in the scriptorium of the monastery called St. Mark's, the legendary Abode of Jesus the Pharisee—I froze for a long time, unable to cross it.

For centuries the story had been told of the most ancient of all the Christian monasteries—The Abode of Jesus the Pharisee, founded by the Apostle Mark himself on his last mission south from Alexandria. There, atop a mountain in the belly of the wilderness somewhere in Sudan or Ethiopia, a small group of monks who called themselves the Sons of Melchizedek lived according to the true teaching of Jesus. Like the Fountain of Youth or Noah's Ark, this mythical place had been sought by countless pilgrims, crusaders, explorers and scholars, all in vain. By the time I heard of the story of the Abode it was a nearly-forgotten legend; I could not find a soul at Yale or elsewhere who believed that the place had ever really existed.

But it did exist, of course; it existed for a single reason: to patiently await my arrival. The Abode of Jesus, the sanctuary of the Truth: a little joke on Mary McAllister by that all-time trickster, God, whose kingdom is forever shut to me. God, for whom I write these notes: the confession of St. Mary, a love-letter from a bee-stung girl. *Dear God, fuck you. Love always, M.*

To resume: I stood in the scriptorium of the Monastery of St. Mark, the Abode of Jesus the Pharisee; I opened the door that had been shut for nearly two thousand years and entered the chamber where no man had stood since the time of Mark (nor woman ever), and beheld the holiest thing in all Christendom: the real Book of Mark, in the Apostle's own hand.

Now here's the funny part. As I stood there, awash in the majesty of unchanging Truth, infinitely removed in time and space from petty human troubles, exempt from the cares of the modern world, as innocent as a child—in other words, as I entered the bubble of the Kingdom of Heaven and became a perfect moron—at that precise moment the twentieth century was condensing around me like a black hole forming around a collapsed star. John Sundman, that human lightning rod, was stranded on a ledge halfway up the cliff-face below the Abode's western wall, nearly dead of thirst. Ismaila M'Bodj and his friend the Baptist were on the canyon floor below him, making plans to detonate a sixty-megaton thermonuclear weapon. Pascale LaFont was approaching from the east like a slow-motion Seventh Cavalry, bringing the wrath of the nation-state fast upon her heals. And above us all the International Vision satellite hovered in stationary orbit: God's eye, Your eye, made visible, watching.

They are gone now; monastery and book alike. The world could no longer abide their indifference, and so destroyed them. The first time Jesus appeared on this Earth, the old world order neutralized him by crucifying him and building an Elvis cult around his memory. That worked for two thousand years. Then up again popped his holy head, like crabgrass on the lawn at MicroSoft, and again the world responded, this time obliterating him by sheer gravitas: hydrogen bombs, satellites, music-television, x-ray lasers, helicopters, tape recorders, vast reserves of petroleum, the world wide web—the dark light of the entire military-industrial-entertainment complex was focused on his ancient book as a child might, with a two-inch magnifying glass, focus the bright light of the sun on an ant. So the gravity of the millennium was focused on that innocent spot, the unread Book of Mark. And the lens was me.

The Sons of Melchizedek have gone to whatever awaits them after this life. Ismaila is likewise dead, and Pascale, and the Baptist; Johnny Sundman has moved to an island off the coast of Maine. I alone am left, with a child and its own kingdom of heaven growing inside me. And you, what do you have to say for yourself?

—*Show me a coin. Whose head do you see on it?*

—Why, Caesar's, of course.

—*Just so. Therefore render unto Caesar the things that are Caesar's, and unto God the things that are God's.*

A tiresome, sophomoric injunction. But hey, You're the Boss. So for five weeks now I have sat squarely in the world of Caesar, trying to render him his due. But what is it, exactly, that I owe him? A thousand channels, each claiming to have the answer to that question, pass through me on the way to my television. I do not need to turn it on to know what they will say: "Come, little fly; taste this morsel that I have placed here for you on this shimmering gossamer. I will take care of the rest."

Willingly I would taste that morsel, but you will not let me. Twenty-four years ago I set out to render unto God the things that are yours, and it is apparent that I cannot escape your hairy fist until I have done with it. So here I sit, a prosecutor with four accounts: Ismaila's tape, Johnny's novel, Isobel's letter, and my own diary. Time's arrow goes only one way, so I will arrange them in order. You will be the judge of whether these accounts agree or contradict each other, and you alone determine whether I have told the Truth.

And once you have been satisfied, once I have rendered unto you your god-damned penny, after I have climbed down, finally, from Lars's lap—will you then allow me, please, to escape at last from your stupid kindergarten?

What the King of Zembla said, gazing upon Lake Venzig from his tower room:

I am a man, not a dog nor yet a drone, and if, compelled by a chemistry beyond my volition, comprehension or ability to describe I was to find myself at the bar of the *Hotel de la Poste* in a provincial city a two-hour ride by *taxi-brousse* from my toubab palace; and if I were there to meet, at around 8:30 PM in the hotel bar, a charming young woman, as black as coal, as handsome as any woman in God's creation, with brilliant teeth shown reluctantly in a shy laugh, so unexpected and charming in one who nightly plied her trade of fucking; and if I were to spend a pleasant half an hour with her at the hotel bar beneath a mural depicting elephants, lions, bamboo glades and the rest of a natural world long gone from those parched regions to be replaced by sand and drought and piles of trees cut down waiting to be turned into charcoal; and if we were to watch bemusedly the

locals and the tourists, conversing amongst ourselves in some hybrid
tongue, ours alone, with a vocabulary small but yet adequate, entire;
and if we were to speak of the countryside, the music on the juke-
box—African, Cuban, Freemerican—and of the vast vast distance
between my home and hers; and if, this sublime half an hour having
transpired, during which time I might have grown increasingly fond
of this delightful person, my sister under God; and if our conversation
were to have turned in a friendly way where we knew it would, to
fucking, and its commerce; and if after a playful friendly negotiation
(as one might banter with the curbside vendor from whom one has
bought his daily loaf for the last fifteen years), a negotiation that was,
though playful, in earnest, and less conducted with great skill on her
part, her tongue around the beer bottle, as I tried feebly to reduce
her asking price, with no real hope of saving a single centime; and if
we were to then agree to a price (which I had already decided to pay
twice-over after the act), and if I—with gooseflesh, pounding heart,
light head and a weakening in the back of my thighs—were to walk
to the hotel desk and engage a room, ostensibly for the night; and if
we were to then have walked silently up the stairs together; and if at
the landing of the second floor she were to have gently taken my hand
in hers, as a schoolgirl might take the hand of a too-shy prom date;
and if, upon reaching room 336, and entering the room, and having quickly shed our clothes—my bluejeans, workboots and T-shirt
clumsily torn off; her blue indigo flowing blouse and wrap-around
skirt melted, liquefied, as graceful as a waterfall—; and if, naked, we
had stood and hugged, and kissed, as lovers, not as whore and john;
and if then, deftly but somehow shyly she had placed a condom on
my cock outstretched before me, plaintively like a child reaching,
reaching; and if, then, as we lay on the bed I quickly placed myself
on top of her, as lover, not as client; and if she took me in, and as I
turned my head away she were to grab my face and pull it to hers,
our tongues wrestling for domination; and if we were to fuck with a
frenzy, a passion, a heartfelt passion, hers as well as mine, fucking as
if our lives, our very souls depended upon it—if all this, if all of this
were to have happened, such an imaginary scenario can be imagined
to have happened, then, surely, certainly, if she were to have asked
me, just as I was about to come, if she were to ask me, with her hand
on the condom, to ask me in our own private one-hour-old language
"Can't we get rid of this?" then surely, for a thousand reasons I would
have said, "No, we must use it." And if she were to have taken it off
anyway, and thrown it on the floor, saying "Come on now, finish what

you started," then surely I would have gotten up, sat up, perhaps even jerked off to satisfy the need, but never, never, would I have said "Alright" and emptied my very essence into her waiting womb.

But suppose, just for the sake of argument, suppose I had. Suppose that I had committed this imaginary act, and that shortly later I had done it again, and once more, a third time, for good measure. And suppose that then we had said farewell.

If we suppose all that, then certainly, without a doubt, if it were to have happened that upon my return to that very same provincial capital three years later, I were to have seen that self-same woman, older, tired, filthy, blank, begging at a curbside with a filthy two year old child—boy or girl; it is hard to say which—sitting beside her, a lovely filthy child the color of cafe au lait, a cold child saying to her mother, *enna boubi,* it's cold: If, solely for the sake of argument, we conjecture all this, then, then, then, then, certainly, without a doubt I would have gone to her.

I don't know what I would have said, or done, but I would have gone to them. That is a certainty. It is impossible to conceive otherwise. It is quite literally unthinkable that I would have averted my eyes, waited a moment, turned back to steal one more guilty glance, then turned on my heel, walked to the trainstation, taken a train five hours to the Capital, taken a taxi from the trainstation to the airport, and returned home to Freemerica after a five year absence, never to go back to Sahelia again.

And then I left the room. My intention was to find the highest spot in that dread castle, and throw myself from it. I looked for Dr. Witold, but he was gone.

There was a noise coming from upstairs. I followed the steps. Atop the stairs I opened the door.

It was a child about five or six years old. I cannot say whether boy or girl; sometimes it is hard to tell at that age. The hair was cut short in a kind of pixie cut, and the clothes were overalls over a blue T-shirt. The feet were bare. Let's say it was a girl.

There was a light on the floor, a fluorescent light—that is to say, a ceiling fixture that had been placed on the floor. The attic room ran the entire length of the great hall, perhaps sixty feet, and it was at once evident that a restoration was underway. There were paint cans, brushes, drop cloths, piles of sheetrock, buckets of joint compound, paper tape, hammers, nails, putty knives, saw horses, extension cords, staging planks, cordless drills, a radio, old floor lamps with floodlights in the sockets pointing straight up at the peaked ceiling (half repaired), two brooms (one a flat straw broom—a Shaker invention; one a pushbroom), two Rubbermaid trash barrels, a dustpan, a fan, a bag of Plaster of Paris, ripped open; a bag of Plaster of Paris, intact; a circular saw, a pile of two-by-fours, a table saw, a sixpack of Coca-Cola, two crushed cans of Diet Pepsi, one can of Tab; screwdrivers (Philips and flat head), a package of Phillies Sports cigars, a doll, a coloring book, several battered notebooks, food containers from a Chinese restaurant, a level, a pile of debris, a coffee pot, and a poster of Brad Pitt. And placed along one wall there was a sign, or rather a crudely-lettered side of a cardboard box labeled in bright red marker that said "Welcome to the Attic. Future home of Eastboro Community Art and Dance."

I would like to say that the child was coffee-colored, but in fact she was white; that is, Caucasian, and her hair was a darkish blond. She noticed me there in the doorway and looked at me for half a second, then, bored, she turned away.

"Mom, watch this," she said, and turned a cartwheel over the light fixture on the floor. As she landed she lost her balance and nearly landed in an open paint bucket. It was only then that I noticed the woman in the dungarees and sweatshirt at the other end of the hall.

"That's enough," the mother said, and her voice reverberated. "I don't want you doing that, you will spill the paint. I've already told you three times. Come on; it's time to go."

The mother looked at me, and I at her; neither said anything.

"Let's go," she said again, "it's late and I'm tired."

The child said, "I can do two at once."

"No," the mother said.

The child ran around to where she had started her approach on the last cartwheel and ran at the light again. Again she did a cartwheel, and her hair hung down over her face for the briefest instant, and the light shone upon it. And she turned immediately into a second cartwheel, barely missing the paint bucket. But as she completed her second spin her foot caught the edge of another open paint pot, one that I had not seen, and it spilled, sky blue, all over the floor. The child fell hard and landed on an elbow.

"God damn it!" her mother said, and the child began to cry as the mother walked quickly to her, crossing the thirty feet in about six seconds, as I stood motionless.

"Don't cry," the woman said, wearily, when she got there. The child was still sobbing, and as she put her arms around the woman I saw the paint quickly spread to the woman's blue jeans and sneakers.

"Come on," she said. "Let's clean it up." Then she looked up at me, with that woman-to-unknown-man look used in these situations that clearly says, Identify Yourself: Friend or Foe.

"Ah," I said, "I was just curious about what was going on up here. I live across the street, and I've noticed the lights on a lot." Lame, but true.

She didn't say anything, but looked from me back to the child. The only civil thing for me to do was to leave, which I promptly did.

I signaled back to the woman, "Friend," then turned, walked out the door and down the stairs, out the main entrance and down the road towards my house.

So, what did it all mean?

I don't know.

Was this child my own? No. Yes. What child is not my own? And your own?

Did this paint-covered cartwheeler shame me back into sanity? Yes. Did she shame my cock down to human size? Yes. Did she resolve all my hang-ups, sexual or otherwise? No. Did she talk to me? No. Did she smile at me? No. Did she in any way communicate with me? No. Was she a vision of beauty? That's hard to say. She looked like any other child. Was she obnoxious? Pretty much. Was she charming? Yes and no. Did she undo the inequities of the world? No. Did she provide any insight into the fate of humanity in the face of our insanely unjust and dangerous divisions of work, health, wealth, property, opportunity, knowledge, or fun? No. Was she the reincarnation of Jesus Christ, along with several other lords (whatever their names), the embodiment of all that is good, and holy, and decent and loving and best and divine in the whole universe, galaxy upon galaxy, from the Big Bang unto the end of time?

Repeat the question.

Was that disobedient child doing cartwheels over a lamp into a bucket of paint indeed Our Redeemer, the Messiah, the Compassionate one, the Creator of Heaven and Earth, the Lord of Hosts, The

Way, the Truth, and the Light, the Glory of God *in omnia saecula saeculorum,* World without End?

The answer to that question, at least, is completely unambiguous.

The answer is yes.

What, then, is the Natural Law, and what does it mean to be a True Patriot of It?

Some claim that the Natural Law had an enormous bearing on the formation of the country, our country, Freemerica. Thomas Jeffersoople, the chief Author of the Declaration that We Don't Want to Walk Around With You No More, is said to have put great stock in the concept of a Natural Law. There is, of course, much debate about the authorship and meaning of that document, but as far as I'm concerned, the Natural Law Interpretation rings true.

We hold this truth to be self-evident: That All Bees Are Created Equal.

What is the meaning of Equal? On the Natural Law interpretation, it means just one thing: equal means separate. The concept of Natural Law says that we are distinct, not continuous. We are separate. We are atomic. We have the right to our separateness. That is what the Natural Law means. To the extent that any government, or institution, or condition forces us to renounce our separateness, that government, or institution, or what have you, is unnatural, and you are not bound by it.

It means that you have the moral right to cast off those things that impinge upon your discrete beehood. You have the right to be left alone. You have the right to not have thoughts inserted into your brain. You have the right to keep your private self private.

That is why the True Patriot of the Natural Law says: You may have your satellite, but if it beams upon me I will shoot it down. You may have your pornography, but you may not slip it under my door. You may make all the noise you want, as long as I don't have to hear it. Keep your airplanes from above my house. That is my sky more than the Airline's sky. Who gave it to them? You may have your television, but your waves must stop at my door. I will not have them in my house; I will not allow you to invade me. Leave me alone. This notion is called liberty, and once, once upon a time, it was believed in here. People fought for this notion. They started revolutions for it.

They bombed for it. They killed daddies for it. They were called True Patriots, and we call them the Founding... The Founding Bees.

Thomas Jeffersoople. Patrick Hank. George Washingtoople. Samuel Adamsoople. You know their names.

They are all dead. There is only one True Patriot left. His name is Kaczinsky, the Unabomber. He fights for a Liberty™ that none of us any longer wants. I don't want it. It's too much work.

I am no True Patriot. We don't need True Patriots any more. Given the choice between freedom™ and clear material advantage, I choose material advantage. Given the choice between autonomy and sublimation into the overmind, I choose sublimation.

I sit in the warm summer sun reading the *Weekly Reader.* How I love to check the mailbox every week. The smell in the barn behind me: Automobile parts in grease, chicken feed, cow feed, oyster shells. A bee buzzes by. The spirit of the hive tells us where to be and what to do at any instant.

I wanna be like Mike™! Pass the Gatorade™!

Gladly I surrender, first this touch of my private self, then that, in return for a promise. For a car. A Mitsubishi™. Don't you call me sir! I work for a living.

Emergence. That's my model. Monty, come back! I wish I were still a drone in your hive! Not here on the cold coast of Maine writing a novel about... About what? What is this long long novel about, anyway?

About a child. A child. A cold child left behind. How the memory of a cold rag-clad child saying *"enna boubi"* it's cold, made me start to think one day in Gordon Biersh, and how after that I was useless.

And at night, the drear starry spaces.

With all our might, all our brains, all our cleverness, all our health, all our strength, all our blessings, can we really do no better than this?

And those softballs, I must say.

Vital statistics, fingerprints, blood types, DNA, worries, vulnerabilities, and all my hope for finding a meaning to my lives. Steer me, Overmind, exactly and precisely where you want me to go. Tell me what to think.

Where then is my defense of the Unabomber?

There is none. He's crazy.

I am a liar. I am a coward.

I do not know how to say what I mean.

I accept the plan given to us by the bloated drones of the mega-transnational corporations. I salute the lords of property, and their hired liars and bumsuckers. I preach their Ptolemaic cosmology which proves that the rich are not wedded to the poor but entitled to the dowry.

But still, I continue to work on my floating point board. There is one error left, and it is a beast. But one day I will find and fix that bug. And after I have found and fixed that floating point error everything will become more clear. Then I will know how to say what I want to say. I will be free of sin. I will bring hope and justice into the world. And I will know how to speak to my dear sweet cold daughter that I left behind in Africa in order that I could come home and write a long novel about her.

The Shakers prospered for two hundred years, two hundred celibate years. The foolish notion that they died out because of their celibate ways vanishes under the least scrutiny. If celibacy were going to stop them it would have done so in thirty years, not two hundred. Celibacy did not destroy Shakerism; the World did. The World saw simplicity of heart, ferocity of faith, passionate mindfulness, dignity of work and most of all community, which means absolutely nothing if it is not predicated upon a solemn pledge to leave no child behind, no matter how the child got here. And the World despised what it saw. So now we have many Disneyworlds, but no Shaker villages.

Shakers gone, next stop: Amish. Amish no want television. Them Amish. Must assimilate.

I ask you, Jesus, come into my heart.

As soon as Joe Regal™ sells the rights to this novel to a mega-transnational corporation I am going to leave this island off the coast of Maine and move to Orlando, Florida.

Most creatures have a vague belief that a very precarious hazard, a kind of transparent membrane, divides death from love; and that the profound idea of nature demands that the giver of life should die at the moment of giving. So says Maeterlinck, and it's a romantic view of his, uncharacteristically romantic. But the Shakers seemed to have agreed with him. I myself do not equate sex with sin or death.

And yet...

I loved a woman, once... I mean, I fucked a whore™.

I cannot square the circle; I cannot reconcile the irreconcilable. *Benin xarit ba abadan,* right Todd? A friend for life.

There is only one bug left. I have done many, many, many simulations. We are left with a race condition and the outcome is indeterminate.

With every purchase I make, Freemerican Express™ gives a dollar to the needy™.

Oh, the child is cold. Summer, winter, spring, fall. So cold.

Question: Are you responsible for the cold children of the earth?

Answer: Gatorade™. Mitsubishi™.

The profound idea of nature demands that the giver of life should die at the moment of giving. There's the Christ™ story for you in a nutshell, huh Betsy? Not a moment's peace can I find. My soul™ is dead.

And so I go to look for my wife and child, a decade too late, and more. I saw them in the dust; they were Jesus™ and I knew them not. I have no illusions about my chances of finding them, nor about the chance of doing anything useful for them now if I did. If I find them they will hate me, as they should.

That's it: the end. This is the feeble conclusion to our story-telling machine's first run: an almost-but-not-quite allegory with some clever but fundamentally unworkable conceits, a shoddily-built and inexpensive complicated mechanism, a tale of a man like any other, a geographical amnesiac prey to lust and guilt living on an island off the coast of Maine who is also a brain in a vat and a bee who mistakenly believes that he is a swarm of bees and a Shaker village. Shall we call this then a crafted meta-narrative, a sophomoric indulgence, or a single run of a buggy program? The question is boring. Here is the fact, the one fact that matters: Jesus is among us; he never left. Along with several other lords, numbering in the hundreds of millions. He is living in the piss and shit in the hell-hole of the earth. He is hungry, he is dirty, and, *omo booby,* he is cold. He is getting mighty pissed off. And I am going to join him.